THE DEFIANT ALPHA

WEST COAST WOLVES, BOOK TWO

SUSI HAWKE

Copyright © 2020 by Susi Hawke

All rights reserved.

Cover Design by Cate Ashwood Designs

Editing by MA Hinkle, LesCourt Author Services

Proofreading by Lori Parks, LesCourt Author Services

Formatting by Leslie Copeland, LesCourt Author Services

No part of this book may be reproduced in any form or by any electronic or mechanical means, including information storage and retrieval systems, without written permission from the author, except for the use of brief quotations in a book review.

THE DEFIANT ALPHA
WEST COAST WOLVES, BOOK TWO

An unwanted alpha and omega long-presumed dead… fate has a way of righting old wrongs.

Stolen from his mother's arms and reported stillborn at birth, "Thirteen" has spent nearly twenty-one years in structured captivity with other stolen omegas. His brothers. A few have disappeared over the years, but twelve remain. An even dozen omegas, each with a secret superpower.

Working together under the light of the full moon, their combined gifts help Thirteen escape—he's their only hope of finding outside help to rescue them all. Except Thirteen is injured and nearly dies as he flees into the night. Collapsing on the side of a desert highway with the sound of a rumbling motorcycle in his ears, Thirteen is sure all hope is lost.

Until it's not…

Found by his true mate, Thirteen is saved—and mated—before the full moon begins to wane. Buckle in for a heart-filled adventure. Omegas are rescued, babies are made, a pack finds its heart, and a birth family is reunited with the one miracle they never could've dared imagine possible.

The West Coast Wolves is an mpreg series about five alphas. A small pack of bikers who spent years riding the highways and helping those in need until fate gave them each a pack to lead. The second in series, this 50k full-length novel is Lucian's story. Prepare yourself for a few tissue moments, lots of laughter, and a birth scene you won't soon forget. But then again, this is a Susi Hawke book so what else can you expect? Possible trigger for child abduction, betrayal from a medical provider, and off-page mention of stillbirth.

A NOTE FROM THE AUTHOR

This book is two months overdue from my original intended release and came after nearly three months of no solo writing due to health issues. After so long off, I had a hard time getting back into the groove, but once I did? Wow, magic happened, and this book came to life for me.

At the end of book one, I kinda wrote myself into a corner unless I wanted Thirteen to be trafficked somehow. Why else would a precious, rare omega not have a name? Thanks to my friend Sammi Cee and a late night brainstorming session, the plot began to take shape.

Before I tell you about the dark, I want to reassure you most of the triggering things happen off page. Aside from the violence of bad guys getting dead, as they should in a shifter book, this is a sweet story at its heart. There are tissue moments, but there's mostly enough fluff to leave you smiling. Also, beware of a birth scene that is sheer farce because nobody can plan when labor happens. If they could, they surely would've picked a different time and place for this one.

Now let's talk triggers. So... here's the thing. This book has three main trigger warnings. The first is for medical abuse. By this I mean where the doctor a person should be able to trust at their most vulnerable is the one who does the most harm. The second is for kidnapped and trafficked children, because that's hard to think about. The third is the most important, and this is stillbirth. While it doesn't actually happen in this book, there are characters who believe it did and suffered over it.

If you or anyone in your family has gone through the loss of a baby, whether from miscarriage, stillbirth, SIDS, or any of the million other scary things that can happen, I want to say that my heart hurts for your pain.

For those interested, I've long been an enthusiastic supporter of angel gowns. These wonderful people take used wedding, prom, and formal gowns and make angel gowns and hats for grieving parents in local hospitals.

The west coast chapter I would normally suggest, since it's in the area where the book is set, is no longer in need of donations. However, I found two sites that touched my heart if you're interested. Or if you live across the world, a simple google search for angel gowns will point you in the right direction for a local group. Here are two I found in the US, and there are more all over the country:

http://www.angelbabiesma.org/angel-gowns-by-angel-babies.html

https://thelittlestangelsgowns.com/

Thank you for choosing my book. If it warms your heart, I hope you'll take a moment to leave a review. Nobody can describe a book better to a reader than one of their own, not even the author.

xox, Susi

ONE

"THIRTEEN"

Present Day...

I INSTANTLY CAME AWAKE when I heard footsteps on the cement sidewalk outside my window, a sound so expected I kept the time by their passing. Closing my eyes, I focused on the tread. Heavier than last time, with a barely noticeable difference each time the right foot lowered with its slightly more metallic thunk. The steady plonk-thunk-plonk gait told me not only was it now midnight, but Jones was working.

The shifts changed twice a day, at noon and midnight. Six large alphas, always around, patrolled once an hour to ensure nobody got in—and none of us got out. This was nothing new, a fact of life I knew since my earliest memories. The day shift guardians were slightly nicer, but the night crew was to be avoided if possible.

Especially when Teacher and his two assistants were absent. Or any of the three support staff members who cooked and cleaned, for that matter. Teacher, and the rest of the people who worked here, weren't any kinder or much better than the guardians, but my brothers and I at least felt safer when they were around. They might speak harshly and force us to obey hard rules, but they didn't stare at us like we were a treat for their taking, as so many of the guardians did.

To my knowledge, the only person here aside from my brothers and our supposed guardians was the night nurse. He wasn't to be disturbed except for emergencies, though we wouldn't have anyway. We tried to avoid anyone outside of our small circle of trust. Anyone working to keep us locked away here obviously wasn't on our side, even if they were merely in it for the paycheck.

I didn't know where the rest of the staff went when they weren't working, but I didn't think it was very far. Another building on the property, perhaps? But then again, I didn't know very much beyond these wooden walls. Asking questions was against the rules, so unless I witnessed something during our weekly walkabout or someone accidentally shared information, I had no way of knowing what I couldn't see, hear, or smell for myself.

Holding my breath, I didn't dare move a muscle until his passing was nothing more than a memory. I knew from experience how these thin wooden walls worked. If I could hear the guardians, they could hear me. Best—safest, really—to let Jones think I was sleeping. The last thing I wanted was to be found awake and vulnerable during the wee hours by any of the alphas, but Jones in particular. Something about his sharp gaze, and the overly familiar way he stared whenever he had a chance, kept me on high alert.

Since it was safe, I was out of my bed in a flash and creeping across the room to quietly double-check the chair I kept wedged under the knob. We weren't allowed locks, and the chair wouldn't stop anyone who really wanted in, but the legs scraping against the cement floor would wake me from even the heaviest sleep. And even better, the sound would echo through this old barn and make Jones—or any guardians with ill intentions—think twice about whatever they might have planned.

"Eleven? Are you awake? Seven? Three?" My brothers and I each had hidden, powerful gifts. We didn't know why, and we weren't asking because it was the one secret we'd been able to keep from Teacher and the staff. One by one, around the time we hit puberty, we'd come into our powers, like my ability to mindspeak.

My brother Six had an intuitive talent we all respected, and he was firm on one thing: Teacher and the staff couldn't be trusted. Master, either, but his shiftiness was a given since this place was under his control. Luckily, we normally didn't see him more than twice a year, when the Missus came along to celebrate one of our birthdays, or for Christmas. Seeing him a third time was bad—it meant one of my brothers would be leaving, never to be seen again, like One, Two, and Twelve.

Blinking back hot tears at the thought of my lost brothers, I firmly pushed my worries about Master and the Missus to the back of my mind and tried again. *"Is anyone awake? If you are, be careful."*

"I'm awake, Thirteen." Seven sounded as sweet and natural in my head as he did when we were face to face. *"What's going on?"*

"Jones is on patrol and heading to your side. After he tried... well, you know... with Five last week, I wanted to warn everyone."

Ten's voice was drowsy. *"It's called a vacation, Thirteen. Except I think he had it backwards because we were the ones getting a break with him gone. Thanks for the heads-up. My chair is under the knob."*

"Mine too," Seven added quickly. *"And if I hear so much as a hint of a scraping chair leg, I'll shift and howl right along with the rest of you. Quit worrying, Thirteen. We know the drill."*

It was good we had a plan in place, but sad we needed one. We figured the combined howls of a dozen wolves echoing through this old barn would make anyone up to no good think twice. It wasn't a certainty, but it was something. *"Okay, then. Good night... stay safe, my brothers."*

Lying back against my pillow, I told myself not to worry. Somehow, some way, everything would work out. Sooner than they knew, these endless nights of my brothers and me sleeping with one eye open would come to an end. The rigid, structured routine ruling our lives would finally be over.

The question was, what came next? None of our powers could tell us. Apparently, even special gifts had their limits. I had my suspicions, but those were based on movie plots so they probably weren't right. When we'd asked Six, he said his intuition only said nothing good came when one of us was taken away. Eight had psychic abilities, but he needed to touch a person to get a vision. Since he couldn't risk touching a staff member, let alone Master himself, the gift was useless to us.

Unfortunately.

The problem was, I had the answer we'd speculated about for so long. I'd learned it was almost time for me to discover the future Master had planned for me. I was simply glad Six hadn't asked the questions I'd seen brewing in his eyes over dinner.

I hadn't told him, or any of the brothers, about what

Teacher wanted when he'd pulled me aside after our morning lessons. Or why I'd avoided them all afternoon, spending time in the meditation chamber. How could I tell them the news when I was still processing it myself? Tomorrow would be the time to let them in. Today had been for acceptance... and planning.

This morning, Teacher's dark, hooded eyes had sparkled with avarice, the lone giveaway how my leaving would in some way benefit him. He'd somberly explained it was time for me to find my mate. The alpha I'd been raised to serve.

When I'd asked who my alpha was, he'd shrugged and said it depended on who bid the highest. His answer perplexed me until he'd explained about the mate auctions, where no one but the wealthiest and most prominent alphas could select an appropriate omega. He said this was the way of things for omegas, and questioning tradition or fate wasn't for the likes of me.

I'd kept a poker face, but I was definitely questioning. If it was tradition, then why was I only now hearing of it rather than during any of the deportment and shifter history classes I sat through over the years? I knew all about pack hierarchy, although I'd never seen a pack for myself. I could serve a dinner for the highest ranking officials and use the correct fork so as not to shame my alpha. I knew how to dress, how to walk quietly but with proper posture and always a few steps behind my future mate.

But this? Being sold to an alpha not of my choosing? The idea certainly hadn't ever come up in any discussion. At least now I had an inkling what happened to my lost brothers. However, I really had no memory of One, and Two had been taken when we were too young to even know our letters yet, so hopefully he'd been part of another kind of auction. I didn't want to consider otherwise, for him or the other two removed from our small, cloistered family.

"Thirteen, you still awake?" Another, newer voice in my head startled me out of my thoughts. My first and only friend outside the walls. We'd never met in person but had shared many long conversations over the past year.

"Unfortunately. Why aren't you sleeping, Alex? Do I need to scold you again about the importance of getting enough rest?"

Alex's nocturnal activities had brought us together in the first place. One night, I'd heard the howl of an unfamiliar wolf, closer than anyone had ever come to our hidden residence. I hadn't expected him to hear me when the random thought *"Who are you?"* flitted through my mind.

But then he'd answered, reasonably wondering why my voice was in his head. Somewhere in the explanation, he'd gotten the entire story out of me. Since then, Alex had one agenda—helping me and my brothers find freedom.

"Dude. Lay off the lectures. I love you like a brother, but I get enough shit from my mom. I'm a twenty-one-year-old man. It's normal for me to want to get out when I can. Which you'd know if we could ever free you."

Chewing my lip, I squeezed my eyes shut, as if it mattered in an already dark room, and considered how to respond. He'd be on board with the plan. The problem was keeping him from overreacting and trying to bust in too soon. His chivalrous tendencies would not help either of us, which was why I never let him come close enough to see our guards. Or, more importantly, for them to see him.

"About my freedom… I have good news and bad news. It's time to put our big escape plan into place. But I need your word you won't leave the hilltop or come within view until it's time."

"Seriously? Hell yeah. Hit me with the good, and the bad won't matter. Just wait until I get you free. We're going to have so much fun. I've been stashing cash for months, and my folks bought me a new car for my birthday. I figure we'll put some mileage between us before getting one of the local packs to come free your brothers. It's gonna be great. If everything goes as planned, I'll be introducing you to the bright lights of the big cities before you know it."

I smiled at the cocky assurance in his tone. "Focus, Alex. The bad matters because I now understand why they won't let us leave."

His wolf growled, the sound reverberating through my head. "You only now understand? Clearly, you're worth money. Look, I've never asked the obvious because I didn't want to put you on the spot or make you feel weird. It's rare, but it's the single sensible explanation. Thirteen, are you an omega?"

Huffing a breath, I sat up quickly, hugging my knees as I rocked back and forth. "Y-yes? I didn't know it was rare, though. My brothers and I are each omegas, according to Teacher. He explained it during our health classes when we were younger. I'm not awfully different from anyone else, am I?"

"Umm... I literally just told you. I mean, you're not so different, I guess. Except for being a guy who can have babies. That's where the rare part comes in. And, unfortunately, why you're worth money to the wrong people. Think about it—how much would someone pay for a unique male who can carry his own young?"

Huh. I would've thought it was our powers. Although maybe Alex didn't know all omegas had the powers we did—or at least the ones I knew. Was it possible he thought I was unique? If so, we'd definitely been smart to keep it hidden around here.

"You're getting lost in thought again, dude. We've been over this—think on your own time. Not when your awesome friend Alex has made his appearance."

"Again with the cockiness." Honestly, it was one of my favorite things about him, though I would

never admit it. His head was plenty big enough already. Laughing, I made myself focus like I'd asked him to do. *"Sorry, the idea caught me off guard. Where were we?"*

"You're stalling. Knock it off. I promise not to freak out and go charging into your little compound. Just tell me what you don't think I want to hear so we can get into the good part where we plan how to get you out of there. Omegas are supposed to be protected. I can protect you. I'm not an alpha, but I am your friend."

His sweet words warming my heart, I breathed in deep and nodded to myself for encouragement. *"So, if I'm as rare as you say, things make a little more sense. Teacher told me I'm leaving on Monday for a Mate Auction. Apparently, auctions are the traditional way for someone like me to get the worthiest alpha."*

"Tradition, my ass." Alex's voice exploded in my skull. *"No. While I wasn't raised in a pack, I have plenty of friends who were. For most wolves, we pick someone we like and get our parents' approval if we're too young. Unless we're lucky enough to meet our true mate, but fate's a crapshoot."*

"True mate? What? Let me guess, they love you truly? No... I know. They're true blue and faithful forever?" I played like I was joking, but I adored the idea of finding someone who would love me for me and never leave. Protect me from ever being hurt again? Um, yes please.

"Yeah, you get the idea. Imagine someone who's your

perfect match, who loves you from the moment they see you and catch your scent, and who will never hurt you because it would cause them too much pain. And you feel the same because your wolf recognizes their scent as mate. Bing-bada-boop, instalove and happily ever after."

"Seriously, Alex? So easy? My nose knows and I'm living a fairytale?" I was ready to believe, but I needed to clarify the details so I could share the fantasy with my brothers later.

Alex's warm chuckle made me smile. *"Seriously. If you can wrap your brain around it, there's the myth. Except it's not really mythical so much as hard to find."* Alex sounded wistful, as if the idea wasn't so bad to him either.

"Huh. Well, if I absolutely have to have a mate, then I'd want one of those. Not some rich alpha who would bid for me in an auction. Do you think the fates were nice enough to make one of those mates for me?" I hated how needy I sounded, but this talk of true mates was making me feel lost and lonelier than ever. Voices in my head, or even the company of my brothers, didn't keep me warm every night I spent on a hard cot in this tiny, cold room.

"I don't know, Thirteen. I hope so... but while the fates might be nice enough to create your perfect mate, they don't usually go out of their way to bring you together. And as for you getting a mate who buys you? Not on my watch. We're getting you out of there before you're taken. Fuck me, I bet the whole reason you guys were kept in there was to sell you off one by one. I'm glad I met you and can help make sure it doesn't happen. Yeah... they can go fuck themselves with a fully loaded bag of dicks if they think they're auctioning you off like a damn cow."

His righteous indignation settled and soothed both my heart and my wolf. Neither of us liked thinking of ourselves as a commodity, let alone how the practice might be considered a tradition among our kind. As for the true mate stuff, I'd save the idea to ponder after I'd tasted freedom.

"Glad to hear it, Alex. Since we've solved the mystery of why my brothers and I were raised here in captivity, it gives me great pleasure to thwart their plans. So what do you say? Think you can help me escape tomorrow night?"

"Tomorrow night? Holy shit, we're moving fast." He paused long enough to realize why urgency was key. *"Oh, snap. You said you're leaving Monday, right? And today's Saturday. Fuuuuck. Okay, let's do this. I can handle a distraction and probably get at least half of your guardians away from there if that'll work? Plus, I can get my friends here as backup. If you don't mind me having them loop in their pack alpha, I'm sure we'll have even more people here to help."*

"I know you've mentioned distracting them in the past, but I don't think you understand how powerful they are. And with plans in place for me to leave, a distraction will probably make them more suspicious. Trust me, Alex. I don't want to risk any of your friends. They won't fight as wolves unless necessary. At least, I don't think they will, since every one of them carry guns. No, I have a better way."

Alex was quiet. *"Listen, I get what you're saying. But there's stuff about me you don't know yet. Believe me when I tell you I'm probably the best person to help you because I'm more familiar with this area than you know. I should've told you sooner, but I was scared you wouldn't trust me."*

"Save your secrets until we meet in person, okay? I promise nothing you can tell me will affect our friendship." I really hoped I was correct. My brothers hadn't liked the idea of me mindspeaking with an outsider, but Six's gut said Alex was okay.

"Promise? Swear you won't hate me, no matter what?" My cocky friend sounded like a scared little boy. So vulnerable and worried, in fact, my heart melted and only confirmed I was right to trust him.

"I can easily promise you as much. Whoever you are, wherever you come from, you aren't the person who put me here or plans to sell me. Enough sentiment. Let me tell you what I have in mind. Tomorrow night is our monthly run. The moon will be full, and none of us broke a rule, so we'll be allowed to shift and run around our yard. As long as we don't go up the hill or leave the fence line, we can have fun for a couple hours."

"And where are your guardians while you're out there? Are they running with you or what?"

"No, I don't think they're allowed to. They space themselves around the yard, armed and ready to shoot if we try to make a break for it. So, I plan to."

"Wait. You want to run away while armed men are literally watching to make sure you don't? No, I think we need to work on a different plan."

"Trusting goes both ways, Alex. You're not the only one with secrets, but the ones I'm keeping aren't mine to share. Believe me when I tell you my brothers are capable of covering for me while I slip away. It wouldn't work if we all tried, but one can be managed. Unless something unexpected happens, my plan should go off without a hitch. Once I get my brothers involved, it'll be smooth as pudding. Nothing will go wrong, you'll see."

Alex groaned so loudly, I would have sworn he was sitting beside me. *"Dude. I know you were raised in a bubble, but everyone knows you don't tempt fate. Like, for real, though. And you call me the cocky one. Shit, now I really am worried."*

"Relax," I laughed softly, hoping to dispel his concerns. *"I'm not being cocky. I'm confident. Now, let's run through this from the top so you're prepared for your part."*

Though he groaned again, he at least sounded more at ease. *"Okay, we've got this. Lay this flawless plan of yours on me, Thirteen."*

"Everything will go down right after sunset." As I lay back onto my pillow and continued to outline my idea, I felt surer than ever it would all work out. We'd never once tried to escape before, so they wouldn't really expect it, I didn't think. Cocky or not, I knew my plan was flawless. It had to be. I didn't dare consider the alternative.

TWO

"THIRTEEN"

"I don't know, Thirteen. Your plan is solid, but so many things could go wrong." Eleven frowned, his eyes narrowing as he stared off into the distance, no doubt calculating my odds of escape.

Eight, possibly the sweetest of us and definitely the most romantic, leaned across the table, his eyes shifting right and left to make sure nobody was listening. "I want to hear more about these true mates. I'm trying to imagine recognizing my soulmate by his scent, and, well... That could backfire. Think about it—what if he just got done working out? Total BO, yeah? How awful would it be if you lost your one chance at true love because you couldn't smell his secret awesomeness underneath the sweat?"

With an exaggerated eye roll, Six held his hands up. "Focus, brothers. Eight, we're wolves. You know the difference between the scents of fear and anger. You would recognize any of us in a dark place, even if we were drenched in sweat and any other nasty fluids you can imagine. I think we can agree—if a person exists whose very scent embodies everything good and calls to your inner beast, you will recognize it, no matter how it might be disguised in the moment. Now, can we get back to the important conversation?"

I nodded gratefully. "My escape. Yes. We have plenty of time to worry about true mates later. Right now, we need to think about ourselves. My freedom will guarantee all of yours, hopefully sooner than later." I was doing my best to keep positive. Six had already gone on record about having a bad feeling about tonight.

At the sound of a housekeeper's footsteps outside the dining room, we paused. Six waited until she was gone to continue. "Exactly. So like I was telling you, my gut says this isn't going to work like you think. But I have a stronger feeling of dread when I consider not trying."

I perked up. "Are you in?"

Closing his eyes, Six took a deep breath before slowly nodding his agreement. "I'm hesitantly giving my approval to the plan and suggesting we work together to help Thirteen tonight. If we all want to go with him, we have the powers necessary, but my gut says joining him now is the wrong choice. A single wolf—or a pair, I suppose, when we include our brother's mysterious friend, Alex—has a better chance of blending in and finding help than every one of us together."

Eleven appeared horrified at the idea. "Good gracious, yes. The logistics alone of keeping track of us out in the wild would need to be considered. But I don't even care to imagine the statistical chances of a small pack of wolves escaping undetected. We don't know what lies on the other side of the surrounding hills. No, I still don't care for the odds of a pair of wolves making it, but at least those are calculable."

With our brother finally calmed down, Five rested a

hand on his arm. "We're all stressed and worried about this, Eleven. It'll be okay, though. I think Six would know if it was going to end in complete disaster. He said things won't work out as planned, but he also said it's the best idea." Turning to me, Five smiled gently. "I vote yes too, and I would beg you to try your best to stay safe and not get hurt."

One by one, the rest of my brothers chimed in with their yes votes and more words of encouragement—and more than one breath of concern. Altogether, whether it worked or not, my plan was a go. Help from the two most essential brothers, Seven and Four, was the only thing I absolutely needed to get away. Still, I felt better about leaving them behind if we were in agreement, and having them on board would aid my escape.

After dinner, we were sent to our classroom for our evening quiet time of reading and meditation before Teacher finally came in. He was a short man with mean eyes who made himself seem larger by ruling us with an iron will and a loud voice. I was so on edge; keeping my scent from betraying my anxiety took everything in me. From a lifetime of experience, I knew Teacher would seize any excuse he could find to withhold a reward, especially our monthly run. He was the one flaw in my plan, the only possible impediment to my getting away without detection.

The shiny top of his bald head reflected the florescent lights as he looked around the room. Lips curled, he gazed into each of our eyes, searching for any infractions. We knew how to play the game, though, and sat up straight with meek, humble expressions. After a long, interminable silence, he finally grunted and motioned for us to rise.

"Gentlemen, you've managed to surprise me. Either you're growing up, or you're finally realizing you have no power here. I didn't expect any of you to make it a full month without receiving a demerit. You've earned a privilege. Single-file line. You will walk as gentlemen to the exit, not shifting until you cross the threshold. While in your animal form, you will maintain this line while you take a walk around the property. You will follow the path and conduct yourselves properly at all times. You will be allowed three laps, and then you will return the same way you entered. Any deviation will bring an abrupt halt to your evening constitutional. Any questions?"

As trained, we politely waited long enough for anyone to speak up before shaking our heads. With no further excuse to stall, Teacher grunted and led us toward the exit.

When I heard Alex in my head, only years of mind-speaking helped to maintain a poker face while holding my place in line and shuffling along. *"Thirteen, I'm in position. Is everything a-go? I see the guards out here with guns, so I'm assuming you're on the way?"* The nerves in his voice mixed with excitement. I could easily imagine him being as on edge because of the danger of our upcoming adventure as I was. Anyone would be.

"We're coming out now. I'll be the wolf near the end of the line, with two behind me. Keep to the plan. I've got this on my end." As I got to the door, I untied my robe and allowed it to slip off, then shifted. The same way I had for Eleven, Fourteen waited for the working housekeeper to snatch up the fabric and set it on the bench outside before he followed in my footsteps.

Different conversations in my mind were like separate channels on the televisions we'd seen in old movies Teacher showed us but never experienced for ourselves. Each week, we obeyed every rule, did every chore, followed every lesson and basically walked on eggshells so we could earn our beloved weekend movie reward.

Using our classroom projector, Teacher would play an approved film of his choosing and we'd get to lose ourselves in another world for two hours. It was the best part of our life here. Like with anything good, we'd lose it if he knew we liked it, so we had to pretend to be unaffected and treat each movie like a lesson we'd be tested on later.

My brain snapped back to the moment at hand. It was time to focus. My brothers were excitedly chattering on one channel in my mind while Alex encouraged me on another. Since giving proper attention to both at the same time wasn't possible, I focused on steadying myself and preparing for departure.

I cleared my mind and put one paw in front of the other until we made it to the small growth of bushes and trees directly across from the old barn where we lived. It was not merely at the foot of the hill, but the sole place on our approved path where my escape would work.

Heart racing now, everything in me torn between needing a hug from one of my brothers and tearing off at a run before it was time, I had to remind myself to be cool. *Left legs forward. Now the right. Keep it together. You've got this.*

Seven interrupted my pep talk, the stress in his tone quickly grabbing my attention. *"Thirteen, I'm stepping out of the tree zone now and pulling the shadows together. The yard will be dark for a few seconds as Fourteen emerges. Tell him to wait until Four projects the fake you. Slip out beside him into the deepest of the shadows and make a run for it."*

I didn't bother reminding him I already knew the plan, since I was literally the one who came up with it. Sarcasm had its place, but not when we were all keyed up. *"Got it, Seven. I know you can't look back, but Four has been projecting my holographic twin since we entered the bushes.*

Make sure you let him know later I give him credit for keeping the hologram perfectly in line behind Eleven. I need to talk to Fourteen now, but until we meet again, remember I love you. Tell everyone to stay safe until I get back with help. We don't know how long it will take, and everything will fall apart when they realize I'm gone."

The plan was for a pack of barking dogs—again, courtesy of Four's gift to project images and distort sound—to interrupt the walk. While the dogs ran through the yard barking, my brothers would break formation, and Four would allow my hologram to fade. Everything would go down fast, probably before I even cleared the top of the hill. We hoped the distraction would delay the discovery of my disappearance and provide an excuse my brothers could use to feign ignorance. With any luck, Teacher would think I'd freaked out and run off in terror. And while they were hunting on the east side of the property where they'd think I'd gone, I'd be headed west.

After a quick check-in with Fourteen, who reminded me to pay attention to the world around me and try not to get caught, I merged into the shadows Seven had gathered, while Fourteen followed my fake self along the path. To make sure no one was gazing my way, I hazarded a quick glance at the guardians before taking off at a run.

"Holy shit, is that you, Thirteen? Your dark fur is blending in great. Lucky some clouds drifted overhead or something. I swear the hill down there wasn't so shadowed a few minutes ago." Alex's jubilant voice bounced through my head.

"Yes, this is me. Where are... never mind, I see you. I think. Are you the gray wolf waiting by the tree?" Please, let it be him. Anyone else, and I was done before I'd really gotten started.

Laughter echoed in my mind. *"Of course it's me—who else would it be? Don't answer. Stupid question. It's totally me."*

As I continued running uphill, Alex started out from the trees and met me, his larger wolf easily matching my pace. I didn't allow myself to look back, but this was already off plan, making me nervous.

Trying not to sound too bossy, I couldn't help but chide him. *"What are you doing, Alex? Are you crazy? The two of us will be more easily spotted. You were supposed to wait at the top of the hill. A plan can't work if we don't follow it to the letter."*

Alex chuffed, bumping into my side long enough to swat me with his tail. *"Only if you're a linear thinker, Thirteen. You'll see. Life happens fast, and sometimes you have to roll with changes as they come. Besides, I got sick of waiting up there. I figured it would be more fun to join you."*

I started to respond with a tail slap of my own, but nearly stumbled. Jones, the guard, was a few feet to the left, peeing on a tree and staring the other way. I knew it was him because his camouflage shorts displayed the metallic artificial limb replacing his right leg. I held my breath, praying to anyone listening he wouldn't look over his shoulder.

Except he did—because then came the sound of barking dogs, courtesy of Four's powers of illusion. It all happened in slow motion, or so it seemed. His penis came into view, spraying a stream of urine as his hips swung around. He didn't hesitate before lifting a gun and firing. The shot went wide, missing both of us as Alex and I put on a burst of speed.

"Thirteen, no matter what happens, keep running. Go as fast as you can. Promise you won't stop if I get hit. If you get

hit, I will drag your ass over that hill if I have to. No matter what, you're not going back. I promised to help you escape, and dammit, I'm doing it."

Jones was still firing at us, the impacts getting closer even though we zigzagged.

A bullet hit the ground in front of me, spraying dirt in my face. Like Alex had reminded me, I just kept running. *"You okay, Alex?"*

"So far, so good. Listen, in case we get separated, I need you to know this. On the other side of this hill, we are going to end up at Highway 58. It's called a freeway. Basically, it's a main road, and the cars will be flying by really fast. When you get there, stick to the bushes where you can and to the ditch running alongside. At first, you can go in the same direction of the cars, but cross as soon as there's a gap."

"Why? If town is in the other direction, shouldn't I go there from the start?" I didn't know why I was asking questions—nerves, maybe? But it distracted me from the gunfire. There was a brief lull as he reloaded before the shots began again.

"There are towns in both directions, but leaving a false trail is great misdirection. They won't be able to track your scent across the highway, so stay on the asphalt as long as you can before you get back in the ditch on the other side. The town you'll come across in the mountains is home to a pack. My friend Ford Silvers lives there. If you make it without me, look him up. Ford's Alpha can help you get the rest of your brothers out—he'll know who to call."

I wanted to ask if I could trust them, since apparently being an omega wasn't safe, but a barely stifled whimper and the coppery scent of blood told me Alex had been hit. His running slowed, but not by much. When I started to falter, prepared to turn back, Alex growled while yelling in my head. *"Are you crazy? I told you to run faster, no matter what. Keep going. I'll be right behind you."*

Another shot blasted, and I heard a dull thud and claws scrambling for purchase in the steep hillside. I couldn't help but slow down long enough to peek back, my heart catching. Alex was crawling through the grass. *"Look away, Thirteen. Keep moving, or we did this for nothing. Go now. I promise I'll be safe as soon as I shift. Jones won't dare leave me long enough to chase after you either—he'll be too afraid I died by his bullet. My father would kill him."*

His words alone almost brought me to my knees and ended my escape. *"How do you know Jones, and who the heck is your father? I'm so confused, Alex. All of a sudden, I feel like I don't know who you are."*

"I'm the same friend I've always been. If I'm correct, my father is the one you call Master. Nothing happens around here without his knowledge. I swear I didn't know he had anyone imprisoned at the back of our property, let alone any plans he might have for you. I would've told you sooner, but I was afraid to lose your friendship. And more importantly, I couldn't rescue you if you didn't trust me. Now please, hurry up and go so I can get the medical attention I need before this asshole succeeds in killing me."

"Okay, Alex. We can talk about this later. But promise you'll be okay."

A sharp pain flared in my left butt cheek, followed by a stinging, burning sensation even deeper in the right shoulder. My body hurt so bad I was ready to drop, but when I realized how close I was to safety, a burst of adrenaline struck.

I dove for the bushes at the top, flying through and landing on the other side... precisely on the sore part of my bottom. The momentum kept me going, though, and I slid and rolled down the hill. Wheezing, I sucked in a breath when I finally landed at the base, coming to a stop in a bush filled with sticky burrs. Yelping, I scrambled to my feet, ignoring the fresh burst of pain as I stepped on a nettle.

As badly as I wanted to know if my friend was okay, Alex was no longer responding. Either he'd passed out from the pain, or... I didn't want to think about the alternative reason.

Between the different points of pain, the burning shoulder, the worry, and my overall anxiety, I knew if I didn't keep going, I'd be done for, and my brothers would never be rescued. Their safety, even more than my own, got me moving again.

I'd read about cars in books and seen them in movies. But movies couldn't tell me how different and scary they were in person. Flashes blinded me from the opposite side of the highway, while the cars whizzing past on this side nearly made me jump out of my skin. Everything smelled weird and unnatural. And it was so loud. And bright from their lights. I didn't know how long I ran before a break in traffic, but when I didn't see lights in either direction, I raced across the highway in a shocking burst of speed.

With my heart racing in my chest, I forced myself to hug the edge of the road and stay on the asphalt for a while, running back the way I'd come. On the road with them, the cars were even more terrifying as they flew past, some coming close enough for me to feel the heat from their engines. A loud horn startled me, making me jump sideways into the ditch. I sat there shaking for several seconds, hunkering down against the ground, away from the view of the cars' occupants. Whenever it got dark, I took off running until the light of the new series of cars came up behind me.

I wasn't sure how far I'd gone, but running and stopping

to wait between cars slowed me down. My body grew weaker with every step of sheer torture. I needed to move faster. While I caught my breath, I watched the road. Inspiration struck when I realized half of the cars' lights didn't extend too far onto the side of the road. In fact, the ground beside the ditch was barely lit. The lone downside was the slope, making it a challenging run, especially in my current state. No matter. The only way to freedom was moving forward.

Ignoring everything but the thought of my brothers and the taste of liberty, I forced my body to run. I kept moving for what felt like forever, pushing onward even when my lungs started burning and my heart began pumping too hard with a weird, unsteady beat, pounding super fast, then fluttering.

Later, I promised myself. I'd think about it later. Right now, I didn't dare because the stinging pains in my butt cheek, and particularly in my shoulder, were getting worse by the second with my initial terror fading into bone-numbing weariness.

Still, I pushed forward, running as long as I could until I stumbled over a rock and tumbled sideways, rolling into the ditch. My vision was blurry as the world spun around me. I tried to look up, but I was suddenly too weak to even lift my head. Lying there whimpering, I couldn't help but wonder if I'd made it this far, only to die in a ditch on the side of a human road.

Except I wasn't even in the ditch. I'd landed on the edge, half in and half out with my head hanging down. The blood rushing to it was probably contributing to my current vertigo.

My vision started to go black. I was wondering if this was really it when I heard the rumble of an engine unlike any of the cars I'd seen so far. Powerful like thunder, it echoed through the hills as if demanding to be noticed and admired.

As everything went dark, I wished I had the strength to see the kind of vehicle issuing such a sound. If cars had an alpha, surely this one must be it. Smiling at my own silliness, I let my thoughts drift as I released my grip on consciousness.

THREE

LUCIAN

A month earlier...

DRIVING through the small mountain town of Tehachapi was a trip. Of the mind-blowing variety. With a population barely over thirteen thousand, it was a charming community nestled high in the Southern California mountains. In the past as I zoomed by on Highway 58, I'd barely registered the exit. I remembered coming into town exactly once, and the high price of fuel and snacks sent me right back to the highway. Although, to be fair, it was probably marked up near the interstate to catch the tourist money, not locals. I'd keep an open mind.

Yeah... looking at the area with fresh eyes, I could see myself settling in here quite nicely. It was definitely scenic. The rugged desert was twenty minutes down the highway, while these hills thrived with life. Sure, rocky hills and craggy bush surrounded the highway, but off of it, trees and grass took over. And grape vines. And neat suburban neighborhoods with manicured lawns.

How had a thriving pack kept themselves hidden in

such a small, enclosed town? Given the surrounding mountains, they couldn't sprawl like most places in this state.

About twenty minutes out of the downtown area, I found myself in the Bear Valley Springs neighborhood and better understood. The homes I passed now sat on larger plots. The land was filled with trees, surrounded by hills and the ever-present mountain. If they kept their heads down, a pack would easily blend in. The GPS told me the address was still a couple miles out, even further from town. Another good idea. Maybe this new pack wouldn't be so bad.

While I was trying not to have any expectations, the best way to avoid disappointment in my book, I'd been half afraid of finding douchebags like Bart Macklebee III, the former alpha I'd killed while defending my buddy Matt's packlands.

I hadn't been the only alpha to accidentally inherit a pack. I was simply the shmuck who'd least wanted one. The West Coast Wolves, my biker club and unofficial pack of fellow alphas, were all growing up with packs of our own, it seemed. With everyone else stepping up to their responsibilities, I'd had no choice but to do the same.

At least, I was sticking with that story when anyone asked. Secretly, Matty's growth as a pack alpha had inspired me, and I wondered if maybe, just maybe, I might have it in me to follow in his footsteps with a pack of my own. After a lifetime without roots or family to call mine, it felt like the right time to take a chance on finding some. Roots, anyway. I had a family with my crew. Anything more would be too much to hope for... and if I harbored a fantasy or two in such a direction, nobody needed to know.

It was okay. I knew I could do this, and at least I was still a quick ride to any of my buddies and brothers-in-arms.

But... fuck. I wasn't like Matthias with his purposeful pack management. How he'd accomplished so much in Lucerne Valley in such a short time was amazing. Although having a mate like Eli didn't hurt.

Yeah, Eli had to be one of his secrets. Matty was lucky to have a perfectly sweet helpmate at his side who knew how to organize with the best of them. Not to mention his pack was filled with good wolves, happy to come together and build a better future for themselves. I'd never felt more at home anywhere in my life than I had during my stay in Lucerne Valley.

If I was going to do this thing—be an actual fucking pack alpha—I needed real, down-to-earth folks like Matty's pack. I wouldn't last a day with fake assholes. That, along with habit, was why I was wearing my WCW cut as I rode up on my beast with its spiffy sidecar. The latter was an addition I'd put on so Eli's kid brother could ride safely, but I'd decided I liked it. It gave my old Harley a special touch, set it apart somehow.

If anyone thought I was keeping it on in case Noah, or pups in this new pack, might want a ride at some point... well, they wouldn't be entirely wrong. It was never too early to teach the next generation to love riding.

Focusing on the area again, I pushed my thoughts aside, hunting for my turn when the GPS spoke over my Bluetooth and told me it was coming up on my left. I noticed several wineries before I rolled up at the address our territory chief, the man who oversaw all the packs in our territory, gave me. The man himself was parked in front of a large wooden sign carved with the image of a wolf howling at the moon beside the name—The Drunken Wolf Winery.

Fucking A, awesome. I remembered hearing the pack had a winery, but hadn't heard what it was called or given it much thought until this moment. *Drunken Wolf Winery*... I shook my head, grinning at the audacity. Things were looking up because any wolves chill enough to pick such a name were my kind of people.

Turning my attention back to the chief, I shut off my engine and removed my helmet before climbing off my beast and walking over to shake his hand. Leaning against his truck, hands in his pockets while he watched me approach, the man grinned like the Cheshire Cat.

"Lucian Smith, am I ever glad to see you. I figured it was even odds whether you'd actually show up to claim your new pack or decide the highway held more interest instead."

Gripping his hand, I couldn't help but laugh at his greeting because he wasn't entirely wrong. "TC Woodlawn, I thought I told you I didn't need my hand held for this part, although I'm damned glad to see you. As for the odds, I wouldn't blame anyone who bet against me. Especially if we've met and they know my opinion about running a pack. But here's one thing they don't know—I always keep my word."

Eyes glinting with fresh respect, he nodded as he dropped my hand. "Glad to hear it. I knew I liked you for a reason. If you can't trust a man's word, then what's the point of dealing with him?" Shoving his hands in his pockets, he nodded over his shoulder toward the open gate. "You ready to do this, son?"

If I wasn't, nobody would ever know. Tipping my chin up with a cocky grin, I held my hands out wide as I backed toward my bike. "TC Woodlawn, I was born ready. Anything I need to know before we go in there?"

"How many times am I going to have to tell you and those rowdy friends of yours to call me Ash? Dammit, son.

Quit making me feel old. I'm still in my prime. The first time was respectful. Now you're just being mean."

Winking, I lifted a shoulder in a halfhearted shrug. "If you don't want to feel old, maybe you oughta stop calling a grown man 'son,' Ash."

"Touché, you little shit. As far as things you need to know, I don't have much. I told them what happened over in Lucerne Valley and how their former alpha went and got himself killed. They know you're coming, and I think you'll find they're—"

A golf cart came flying through the gate, taking the turn on two wheels, kicking up dirt and pebbles in the process. Fortunately, it came to a complete stop without hitting either of us, since we were both too busy gawking to react.

The man driving was about my age, maybe a year or so younger but not much more. He hopped off and slipped his sunglasses to the top of his head, appearing every ounce the preppy in beige golf shorts and a pale pink polo shirt. The sockless feet in his matching pale pink chucks amused me.

Still, his outfit worried me until he looked back and forth between us with a welcoming, yet slightly uncertain smile, as if he couldn't figure out who to greet first and wanted to get it right. Despite his fashion choices, the dude wasn't a little rich prick douche canoe.

And hey, I had to admit the pink worked against his bronze skin and coal-black hair. I wouldn't be messing around with anyone in my new pack—even an avowed manwhore like me knew better than to shit where he ate—but if I'd met him in a bar, I would've offered to buy the cutie a drink.

He was still trying to make up his mind when Ash was kind enough to come to his rescue. "Perfect timing, Raul. I was about to escort your new Alpha inside. Now I can leave him in your hands and get going to my next stop. Alpha Lucian Smith, I'd like to introduce you to the Tehachapi Pack Beta. This is Raul Ramirez. Anything you need, this is your guy. And his parents, but you'll meet them soon enough, I'm sure."

Grinning, Raul took the hand I extended, his white toothy smile nearly blinding in the midday sun. I made a point to keep my grip firm but not overwhelming. No need to grind my alpha status in or be a dick, especially if I wanted to start off on the right foot.

"Nice to meet you, Raul. Give it to me straight. Am I walking into chaos since I killed your former alpha, or is the pack okay with my being here?" I figured it was better to address the elephant in the room, namely the now-deceased Bart Macklebee III, before things went any further.

Quickly shaking his head, still smiling, Raul seemed perfectly fine with the unexpected change in leadership. Amusingly, he talked as fast as he drove, dropping information in a huge dump for me.

"No chaos here. Not at all, Alpha. We're ashamed to know what Alpha Macklebee did. To attack another pack is an act of war. We're a peaceful community, so it came as a shock. Sure, a few people cashed out and left, but I think you'll find the majority of us are excited for the change. Alpha Macklebee was more of the governor than a hands-on pack alpha. Not to speak ill of the dead," he paused to cross himself, "but it was time for a change. The Macklebees, from what I know, were never the most involved. My parents are excited and hoping to see us become a real pack, rather than loosely connected neighbors who work at the same place and share the shifter gene."

"Damn, you gave me a bit more honesty than I was expecting at the front gate." I could already tell this was a guy I could be friends with, preppy or not. "How are you guys not a real pack, if you don't mind my asking?"

Ash stood quietly listening, obviously enjoying the chance to learn new information. Surprises weren't something a territory chief looked forward to learning about a pack under his purview.

Raul took a moment to consider his response, making me respect him that much more. "Like anyone else, we have a Gamma Council. But they've had no power. They're mostly there to vote on dispersing funds and deal with municipal issues. We don't have a Delta force, although every adult male is trained to defend the winery when necessary. But, to be fair, we haven't been attacked by another pack in over forty years. Our biggest drama here is when a guest overdoes it in the tasting room. It's... I don't know. You'll see what I mean. We don't have the same connection I've heard about with other packs."

Even though I'd never officially been part of a pack, aside from the West Coast Wolves, I knew what he was talking about. The draw to pack living was the connection and sense of community. A pack without heart was nothing. It was simply a nice enough life spent among a group of people who lived and worked together but shared nothing more.

Strangely enough, learning this completely dropped any lingering reservations. From the sounds of it, the pack might really need an alpha like me. Maybe this would be as good a change for them as I was hoping for.

Since I was shirtless under my cut, I opened the left side of my leather vest and displayed the unmarked skin over my heart, missing the X most other shifters wore. The proof I'd been born a bastard and left unclaimed—a fate considered worse than death to most shifters.

Dropping my hand from my cut, I winked and pointed to the sky. "Seems like someone upstairs is having fun with us, Raul. Dropping an alpha who *wasn't* into a pack who *isn't*... Pretty ironic. But you know what? Let me get the lay of the land, and maybe we can find a way to give me and every one of you the thing we've all been missing out on. First, though, how about a tour?"

Before he could respond, Ash clapped me on the shoulder. "Look at you, already finding your stride, and you haven't even set foot in the gate. I'm anticipating hearing good things from the Tehachapi pack as you start moving forward, Lucian. Now if y'all will excuse me, I'm late for a meeting with the Bakersfield alpha. Poor sucker is fighting the city about water rights again. Can't tell you more, but should be enough to let you know I'm not happy to hear it."

"Good luck, Ash. You go ahead now. I've got it from here. I appreciate you being here to greet me—nice of you." It really was, too. I was never afraid to shoulder my way into any situation, but Ash's presence had allowed me to relax and be myself. Any time I didn't have to pull out a fake, political smile or bluster my way through a pile of bullshit was a win in my book. Plus, I had high hopes for Raul.

After Ash pulled away, I nodded toward my machine. "Should I leave my ride here while you show me around, or is there a better place I can park first?"

Raul thought, then nodded at my bike. "Let me show you where to leave it. Then you won't have to worry. We don't get a lot of crime out here, but we don't have cameras at the main entrance like some of the other vineyards."

Covering my surprise at their security lapse, I went for my bike. "Just show me where. I'll be right behind you."

As it worked out, I was glad to react to the city without anyone watching. The first thing I noticed was the orderly rows of grapes spread out on either side. The buildings we passed were solid gray stone and wood, painted white with dark green trim. Everything appeared clean, neat, and, well, rich. Then we went around a curve, and I came face to face with a house big enough to be called a mansion. Except it was trying to be low-key and cool about it. Done in the same white wood over gray stone as the rest of the property, but with way more windows, the house was gorgeous.

Maybe it was the absence of some big-assed fountain with an angel pissing onto poor, innocent koi swarming below, or maybe it was the TV-ready front porch with its random assortment of unmatched wooden chairs and pots of flowers, or maybe it was simply the way it blended in against the mountain looming in the background. All I knew was it looked like a place where rich people might live but normal folks were welcome too.

Parking my beast and its attached sidecar in the garage Raul pointed out after we'd pulled around to the side was almost embarrassing. Not because I was shamed by my ride —never. Nah, I just sensed this place was meant for fancy cars, worth more than I'd make in my lifetime. But then it felt ordinary, too, when I saw an oil spill in the middle of the garage bay beside mine. Yep, rich but normal. I could definitely see myself living here.

I walked out of the garage, heading to the golf cart, when an older couple approached. Raul slumped over the steering wheel and rubbed a hand over his face before hopping off and coming to my side as they reached me.

Shaking his head, Raul shot them a chiding look. "Mamá, I told you I'd bring the Alpha to the manor when he was ready."

"Hush, mi hijo. Introduce us, por favor." A tall, angular woman, Raul's mother's narrow face was a contrast of sharp points, and a warm, welcoming smile with sparkly, shining eyes. "Ask your father. I was too excited to wait another second." Her husband, a solid man standing a head shorter than his mate, simply shrugged and held his hands out, clearly not wanting to take sides or argue.

I couldn't help but find myself charmed. But then, family interactions always fascinated me. Not having one made a guy curious, I supposed. My own history wasn't a tragedy to me, so I wasn't jealous. Hell, my unmarked chest was a quick way to get in someone's face and dare them to show their true colors. Funny how often trading on it worked for me over the years.

Stepping forward, I offered my most charming smile to the lady. "No need to get too excited on my account, ma'am. Raul was about to give me a tour, but we can certainly spare a few minutes to show some respect to his parents."

Raul looked like he wanted to roll his eyes and call me out for throwing him under the bus, but he didn't know me well enough yet to bust my chops. He swallowed, then smiled tightly. I wasn't sure what he was planning to say, if anything, but I couldn't take watching the little guy squirm.

I laughed, gently pushing his arm. "Chill, Raul. I wouldn't seriously do you like that, man. At least, not before we've gotten to know each other. I know respect is everything in Latino culture, so I decided to mess with you. I figure it's best if everyone knows from the start the kind of alpha I am. Meaning I try not to take myself or most situations more seriously than necessary."

Eyes going wide, he huffed a laugh before shaking his head. His parents cracked up along with us, and bada bing, bada boom, the ice was broken.

Turning back toward his parents, I held my hand out to the mother. "I'm gonna go out on a limb here and assume you're the boss, ma'am. Alpha Lucian Smith, at your service. Lucian works fine, though, and I'm more likely to answer to it."

She gave me a quick onceover with a prim smile and sharp eyes, not missing a thing. "Bueno. Welcome to the Tehachapi pack, Lucian. Enough 'ma'am' business. I am Esmeralda, and this is my mate, Pedro. You will call me Essie for now. Eventually, you'll call me Mamá like everyone else does."

I dropped into my familiar routine of opening my cut to display the unmarked flesh over my heart. "Essie it is, then. Since I didn't grow up with parents, I'm afraid it's a bit late in the day to call anyone Mamá at this point. Y'all probably weren't expecting an unclaimed alpha to lead your pack, but it is what it is."

Rolling her eyes like someone half her age, she snorted and swatted my hand away from my vest. "What, am I supposed to be impressed by your manly chest or decide your worth based on the actions of the people in your past who didn't value it? Their mistake has nothing to do with who you are. Just wait, tough guy. You'll come around. Before you know it, you'll be calling me Mamá and sneaking cookies from the kitchen."

I grinned, liking this lady more by the minute. "I like how you brought the conversation back around to you, Essie. While I give you props for not looking down on me, I do have to ask—where's the pity most moms show me? I mean, don't you feel even a little bit sorry for the poor baby alpha who was left unmarked, unwanted, and unloved by the people who brought him into this world?"

While she cackled, Raul and Pedro simply watched the show, which only made me like this family more. If they could roll with such a crazy introduction, they definitely didn't take themselves too seriously.

After wiping her eyes with the back of a hand, Essie smiled broadly and hooked her arm through mine as she rested her head against my arm, as if she could tell that was as much of a hug as I could accept at our first time meeting. After a few seconds, she patted my arm and stepped back. "You'll do, Alpha. Quite nicely, I think. Our pack needed someone like you to breathe life into it. And you, tough guy, need me more than you know."

"If you say so, ma'am. I mean, Essie." Pausing, I winked, teasing her to show my approval. "Since you've given me a proper welcome, how about you point me toward those cookies you mentioned?"

"Ha, not so fast, young man. Alpha or not, you'll wait for dessert to get goodies. If you haven't had lunch, I'll be happy to make you a sandwich. Otherwise, let my son give you his tour and get you settled in. I have a welcome dinner to prepare. One question, do you prefer pork or chicken in your enchiladas?"

I was tempted to say beef to mess with her, but she looked so damned serious I couldn't find the heart to do it. "Essie, I will happily eat any form of enchilada you set in front of me. But if I have a choice? I'd have to go with pork."

"Bueno." With a nod to Raul, she motioned for Pedro to follow as she headed toward the big house without so much as another word.

Staring after her, my mind went blank for a few seconds before I turned to her son. "What just happened?"

Raul cracked up. "You met Mamá. She's a force of nature. Don't try to fight it. You can't escape her anyway. She runs the Alpha manor, and the three of us live there with you. I have a separate apartment, of course, but we're all on site."

"Good to know, but not unexpected. Most pack Alphas have live-in staff, right? At least, the bosses with big places like this one, from what I've seen. What's up with your dad, though? He didn't say a word." I hadn't realized until this very moment.

"Dad doesn't talk much, you'll find. He manages the vineyard. When he does speak, though, you'll want to listen. He saves his breath for the important things." Leading me over to the golf cart, Raul got back behind the steering wheel and fired it up. "I'm mostly going to give you the scenic route today so you can get the lay of the land. I don't expect you to memorize everything, so don't stress yourself. It'll come with time, especially if you've never lived or worked around the winery before."

The engine was quiet, so we could easily converse as he motored around the property. Thankfully, he drove at a much slower pace, showing me the different outbuildings and whatnot. Everyone we passed waved with a friendly smile, but nobody stopped working. And through it all, Raul chattered away about everything from grape varietals to oak barrels and how many finished cases they averaged per acre.

Between Raul acting like I was the new hire being welcomed to my new job at the winery rather than showing the packlands to his new Alpha and the non-reaction of the pack members themselves, I understood better what he'd meant about the nature of this pack. And damned, but if that didn't go a long way toward making me feel needed here. If I learned one thing during a childhood spent in the shifter foster system, shuffled to a new pack every six months, it was how the best packs operated.

Tehachapi might have had wealth, but they lacked the

most essential ingredient for a healthy pack—the sense of community. After the tour, my eyes were already open, but when Raul led me into the winery's main office where the Gamma Council met me in a conference room, the missing ingredient really slapped me in the face. The authority and confidence of running a thriving pack were completely lacking. These guys weren't warriors who oversaw a Delta force; they were bureaucrats.

After twenty minutes of pie charts, spreadsheets, and other corporate bullshit, one of them shoved a contract at me. I'd had enough. I rested my hand on the thick stack of papers, half wondering which of these guys was most likely to have a roll of antacid tablets in their pocket. Fuck me, my stomach was churning after sitting through even this brief business meeting. Carefully setting the contract aside, I kept a polite smile as I looked around the table.

"Gentlemen, if I may be so rude as to interrupt your presentation? You'll have to pardon my confusion, but I assumed you were the Gamma Council, yet this feels like a board meeting."

Shrugging, John, a blond dude in his mid-thirties, loosened his tie. "You're not wrong, Alpha. The four of us all hold executive positions. The winery is our primary job in the business of running this pack. There aren't many personal issues. Our members keep to themselves and solve their own problems."

The man next to him, a slick Italian guy named Tony with a prominent New York accent, nodded in agreement. "What he said. Yo, we don't worry about what they do in their own homes. We care about whether or not they do their jobs and the product gets handled. And since every pack member has a share in the winery, getting the people to work isn't a problem."

Miguel, the oldest of the group yet still somewhere in his forties, raised a hand with a mild-mannered smile. "Perhaps I can shed some clarity on the situation, Alpha. We're simply doing our jobs as required by Alpha Macklebee. He felt the winery took precedence. Each of us were chosen for the council based on our educational background and ability to manage the business."

I glanced across the conference table, making eye contact with the youngest person in the room. Despite staring me down like he had something to prove, he hadn't had much to say as of yet. Either that, or he wanted to impress me. Hard to tell, especially with a guy who looked twenty-five if he was a day. I figured I'd keep an open mind and a watchful eye since his attitude could go either way. I held his gaze long enough to remember his name before speaking.

"What about you, Ramon? Are you happy shuffling papers, or would you like to be more involved in running the pack?"

Ramon's eyebrows shot up. "Seriously? Alpha outlined our positions himself. I mean, yeah. I wouldn't mind getting out of the office, but not if you want me to start supervising out in the field or working in the warehouse. I'd be down to host one of the tourist groups in the tasting room, but anything else would be a demotion."

Puffing my cheeks out, I cleared my lungs in a loud burst of air before standing and walking around the table. As I moved, I let the Alpha pheromones fly and made a point to touch each of them on the shoulder or cup a hand over the back of their necks while I better explained myself.

"Gentlemen, I've heard enough. While the winery is important, and I have to say you have a real nice operation going here, it's not your primary job. Here's the problem—

you're running this place like humans. Where are your wolves? Where are those lupine sensibilities demanding pack?"

Tony lifted his chin, his eyes flashing with annoyance. "Caring about the business supporting us all doesn't make us less of a wolf than you. Maybe if you read your contract, you'd see you have just as much interest as we do in keeping things running smoothly. As Alpha, you automatically own forty percent. What do you think paid for that nice-ass house you're moving into today? Don't put us down when we're lining your pockets too."

In three steps, I was at his side, gripping the back of his neck with a snarl. "I'm an easygoing guy, but even I won't allow a pack member to disrespect my position."

Instantly, his head tilted to the left, baring his neck in submission. "S-sorry, Alpha. I didn't mean no rudeness, truly."

"Thank you, Tony." Releasing him, I took a step to the right and knocked on the table a few times. "Pay attention, gentlemen. Today is when we start fresh. The day we remember we are a pack first and foremost. The business, while important, can only ever come second to the pack. I'm going to be making a lot of changes around here, so prepare yourselves. Together, we are going to rediscover the kind of pack with a sense of humor who named their winery so appropriately. The Drunken Wolf? I love it. Help me find those people, the ones who didn't take themselves as seriously."

Scratching his head, John looked puzzled. "How can we hold a place of leadership if we have no sense of decorum?"

"Good question." I smirked, tapping my forefinger against the side of my head. "It's all about moderation, John. You'll see, and in a few months, you'll be glad I saved you from spreadsheets and pie charts. I don't care if you guys want to maintain your positions here in the winery, but I'm going to require a more hands-on approach to other pack matters. I'm also going to institute required pack runs and open my home for a weekly potluck. Small changes will get us started. Before we know it, the people here will be pack members rather than shareholders."

Raul had been surprisingly silent up until now. So much so I'd almost forgotten he was there until the sound of a slow clap got my attention. He was grinning like a mofo. "Allow me to be the first to extend the wrist, Alpha. As Beta of the Tehachapi pack, I am both proud and pleased to accept you as my Alpha. Gamma Council, I don't think we need a vote, but if you need one, mine is aye." As he spoke, he got out of his seat and walked over to the open area beside the table. Hitting his knees and bowing his head, Raul extended his arm with his wrist held up for my bite.

The Gamma Council came to life, reeking of excitement. Hell, the air was so charged, I was tempted to open a window. They shared a quick glance before nodding without any discussion. Boldly looking me in the eye, Miguel proudly delivered their verdict. "Alpha Lucian Smith, we the Gamma Council of the Tehachapi Pack accept you as our Alpha." They surged to their feet, rushing over to join Raul and assume the same positions.

I'd never felt more touched in my life. Swallowing and blinking back some allergy-related moisture, I walked over to stand before them. "Thank you, gentlemen. I know your official acceptance is required by tradition and mostly ceremonial, but I appreciate it. As for your personal submission, words can't describe how much your actions have touched me. Together, we're going to build something special here. You have my word on it."

As I took a moment to bite each of their wrists, my body buzzed with the pack connection forming between us. Once I finished here, I'd have to see about sweet-talking Essie into my weekly pack potluck. Food was always a good place to start when forming a family, at least in my book. Hopefully, she wouldn't kill me for announcing it to the Gammas before discussing it with her.

Hopefully.

FOUR

LUCIAN

Present Day

After a month, my new pack was finally starting to feel like one. The weekly potlucks and setting up a rotation of deltas had gone a long way. The Gamma Council had visited Matt's pack over in Lucerne Valley and were acting more and more like pack leaders than winery executives.

Altogether, I was happy with the way things were going. Tonight would be our second official run, another thing to help cement our fledgling pack consciousness. And the reason I was racing home like my ass was on fire.

Honestly, I shouldn't have even gone for a ride today. It wasn't like I'd needed a break or anything, but my wolf demanded it. For the last several days, he'd been on edge. Since tonight was his chance to run free, I'd hoped he'd chill out, but no such luck, so I tried distracting him.

Goddess knew I'd needed to feel the road under me anyway; it had been way too long since I'd been out.

It hadn't worked, though. Even now, when my wolf should have been relaxed and looking forward to the midnight run, the bastard paced inside me, growling and demanding we stay on the road. Keep hunting. For what, neither of us knew.

But nothing short of an emergency would keep me from my pack tonight, so I was heading back to Tehachapi whether my wolf liked it or not. He might not have been happy, but we had our responsibility to our pack. Even if the beast wasn't in the mood, my human side respected our duty.

My mind continued to wander, wondering why I'd been feeling a low-key urgency myself recently. The last time I'd felt this way, like I was on the cusp of a major life change, I'd ended up killing a man a few days later and inheriting his pack. This time felt... *different*, somehow. Like my very life depended on protecting something. S*omeone*. The problem was, in order to defend them, I needed a clue as to what was in danger.

The closer I got to home, the more the hair on the back of my neck stood up, and my stomach clenched. Whatever was about to happen in my life, it was close. My eyes automatically started scanning the road, my shifter-enhanced vision helping me see more of the dark ground off to the sides than a human ever could.

I eased off the throttle and slowed as I came around the first curve taking me higher into the mountain. If I hadn't, I might have missed the brown dog lying half out of the ditch. At this speed, I was able to stop in plenty of time to check it out.

The poor thing looked dead. Hopefully not, though, since I was feeling strangely drawn toward it. Had someone's dog been hit by a car? Or even worse, had an animal been abandoned and left to die? While sickening, such cruelty wasn't unheard of, especially on high traffic roads like this. No matter. I'd always wanted a dog. If this one could be saved, I'd give it a home with all the love its heart could handle, since I knew a thing or two about being tossed aside.

Parking my bike as close to the side as possible with the attached sidecar, I hit my flashers and crossed my fingers no one would come hurtling around the corner and crash into my ride. My headlight lit up the area, letting me see the unprotected stomach and balls of a medium-sized, toffee-colored wolf. Huh. Seeing such sensitive areas on display told me the wolf was either dead or knocked out.

Before I took a step away from the bike, my wolf howled and tried to jump forward. He slammed against my chest, pushing to take over. Fighting him back took more strength than it ever had in my life, and within three more steps, the wind shifted, and my human nose understood what my wolf had already discerned.

This wasn't a wild wolf, and he wasn't dead. This was my mate.

I took off at a run, rushing to his side and frantically checking for a pulse. Between the thick fur and my own nerves, finding the fluttering proof of his heartbeat took longer than it should have.

Even as I breathed out in relief, I felt almost foolish. On some level, I'd known he was alive since he didn't smell like death. No, he smelled like candied ginger and some soft herb I couldn't quite name at the moment. And more importantly, he smelled like... home. Like *my* home. The one place where I would always belong.

His weak heartbeat concerned me, as did the dried blood covering his paws and the ridiculous amount of burrs and nettles matted into his fur. He clearly needed a healer. Sliding a hand under his head, I gently lifted it and brushed my fingers over his muzzle while I considered my next steps.

A human doctor was out of the question, but the one thing lacking in my new pack was anyone with medical skills. The sole epsilon I knew of was an hour away, give or take, in Lucerne Valley.

Shit. Of course I should've thought of Matt's pack immediately. Not only did they have an epsilon, they were better set up to help protect and defend my omega mate than my newly trained deltas. The men in my pack had fighting skills, but they weren't soldiers. Matt sent a couple of his Delta captains over to help with my newly formed squadron, but it was a work in progress. Not until this week had we finally been able to start zeroing in on possible captain candidates to take over when Matt's men left.

Carefully lifting him, I cradled my mate against my chest, shielding his body from further injury. A semi rumbled by, throwing a blast of heated air our way. Seeing the truck reminded me of our vulnerable position, further hammered home as several cars roared past.

Moving carefully, I hustled as much as I dared, carrying him to my bike, where I settled him on the sidecar's floorboard. I snagged a blanket from one of the compartments, tucking it around him as best I could to help protect his smaller body from the wind. I wasn't sure if it would hit him down there, but better safe than sorry.

Once I had my helmet on, I fired up the beast and merged with traffic while I tapped the button for my Bluetooth. As soon as Raul came on the line, I explained the situation and asked him to oversee the pack run tonight. Raul had already proven himself to be efficient and the perfect beta for me, so I wasn't surprised at his easy acceptance.

"No problemo, Lucian. I've got things here. Your mate

comes first. We'll be here waiting to meet him when he's well. I'll let Mamá know—she'll want to light a candle. Be safe. Don't drive like a demon tonight. Remember, getting in an accident will only prolong getting him to a healer." Considering the way he drove, I grinned at his warning, but I appreciated the concern.

"Thanks, Raul. I'll be in touch." After I ended the call, I pushed aside all worries about my pack. For the rest of the drive, I focused on two things—the road and keeping one eye on my mate for any sign of further distress.

The journey was over before I knew it, and I had a moment to be glad Matt had removed the gate separating his property from the rest of the pack, so I didn't have to slow down heading up his driveway. Then I realized Matt had no idea I was coming. Belatedly, I hit the Bluetooth and inspected my phone to call him. A short conversation later, I was already parked and lifting my mate as Matt and Eli came rushing out to greet me.

I barely had a chance to explain and request to see their epsilon before I found the man himself watching from the porch. Isaac, like every other healer-type I'd ever met, looked mysterious as hell and emitted powerful vibes, leaving little doubt of his gifts. I didn't care how long that gray beard was or whether his shirt paired well with his red corduroy pants. I just wanted to know if he was the real deal. Then he spoke in the elevator and made me a believer.

His eyes were kind, even as his words socked me in the gut. "Don't worry. Thirteen is stuck in this form because his wolf is the sole thing keeping him tethered to our world. Your presence will assist in bringing him back. But first, we must take care of his wounds and alleviate much of the pain. All will be well in the end. It's been foretold."

When he referred to my mate as Thirteen, I assumed he

was talking about how many patients he'd seen and couldn't understand why. Maybe to take my mind off the stress while we headed to his clinic?

Looking down at my mate, then back at Isaac, I frowned in confusion. "Why did you call him Thirteen? Do you number your monthly patients or something?"

"Why ever would I do such a thing? No. I called him Thirteen because it is his name. Or rather, the number assigned to this dear, unnamed soul."

Fuck, if my heart wasn't already breaking, hearing that nearly brought me to my knees. My mate wasn't merely unclaimed at birth—nobody had even taken a moment to name him somewhere along the way.

Eli asked the question before I could. "Pardon me for asking, Isaac. But how do you know the details?"

Isaac rocked back on his heels, managing to look bored as he glanced at the small, worried omega. "The same way I know everything. My spirit guide told me." After that, there was nothing but silence. We made it to the clinic area and Isaac had me lay him on the scarred surface of a large wooden table. While he started his examination, I held Thirteen in place, mostly because I needed to touch him, and let my mind drift.

Somehow, not having an alpha scratch an X over your heart was nothing compared to being left unnamed. Maybe the fates knew what they were doing when they matched mates. I couldn't think of anybody better prepared to love and protect this previously unwanted omega more than I would.

And when Isaac said my connection would be the only thing to save him since he was so loosely tethered to our world right now? Damn. My wolf wanted to break free and howl our pain. As badly as I wanted to do the same, I was doubly determined to save my mate. To keep him and hold him close. To love him so hard he wouldn't remember ever having gone without it.

If any of my buddies could hear the sappy thoughts my heart was sending to my brain, they would either keel over from shock or laughter. Either way, they wouldn't believe I was capable of it. Probably. I knew I hadn't known I was this mushy.

Smiling at myself for being so weird, because who wouldn't be mushy at a time like this, I blocked out the rest of the room while I began working alongside Isaac, picking burrs and brushing Thirteen's fur with a soft brush. Isaac handled the physical first, removing a bullet from the right shoulder and tending to his wounded paws before he did anything else.

I had no clue why Isaac lit candles and spritzed incense while he chanted over Thirteen. There was more to the ritual—a rattling stick came out at one point, and a small gong was struck at another—but I barely paid attention to any of it.

My entire focus was on the small, toffee-colored wolf. Isaac guided my hands, resting one on my mate's head and the other on his heart. Placing his hands over mine, he chanted some more. By the time he was finished, I could feel the beginnings of what would eventually become our bond.

Gasping, I looked the healer in the eye. "What kind of sorcery are you using to begin the bond for us? I had no idea such a thing was possible. But yet... I can feel his pain, and if I push deeper, I can sense his sweet soul."

With a sage nod, Isaac managed to appear even more mysterious. "It's not always possible, but the goddess allowed it as she does in certain, desperate cases. Just as you can sense his soul, he can feel yours as well. His unconscious mind will allow his wolf permission to absorb your strength and recognize you as their alpha mate. Sharing the pain will transfer its burden to the stronger mate and help the weaker body find the strength it needs to heal."

"Seriously? Then pile it on. I have wide shoulders and a strong back. I can carry all of his pain." I meant it too, every word.

Isaac smiled, the expression startling and almost gruesome, despite its raw beauty on his weathered face. "And your answer, young man, is exactly why the goddess allowed a partial bond to be put in place. The strongest part of you is your warm heart. I would urge you to remember that and let love guide you through whatever life throws your way. If you lead from compassion, you will never go wrong."

Unsure how to respond, I swallowed uncomfortably and nodded toward my mate. "What happens now? Will he need surgery? Or do we gotta wait and see what happens overnight?"

Shaking his head, Isaac tutted as he turned for the door. "Now we sleep and wait for the boy to awaken. My advice would be to shift and curl up beside him tonight. It will strengthen your bond and keep him warm and allow your wolf the comfort of protecting your mate."

He started to leave, then turned back with one more thought. "You can move him from the table. His body is out of danger now. There's a bed in the corner—feel free to make use of it. You will both rest better there."

Until I found myself alone with Thirteen, I didn't realize Matt and Eli had disappeared at some point. I didn't blame them. They had a newborn sleeping upstairs, along with their two other children—actually Eli's brothers, but

Matt had adopted them as his own. At six and twelve, the boys deserved a happy childhood and needed every bit of the protection a strong alpha like Matt would give them.

When Matt met his mate and found a family in the process, I hadn't thought I could ever be happier. Funny how finding my own mate completely eclipsed my joy for him.

Taking Isaac's advice, I carried Thirteen over to the bed and got him settled before stripping and allowing my wolf to emerge. Isaac was correct, I quickly discovered, as I curled protectively around my mate and finally felt at peace. My wolf and I were in complete agreement; this was absolutely where we needed to be right now.

In this form, I could feel the bond more strongly, smell his scent, and even better, imprint mine on him. It wasn't much, but it allowed me to rest. Using my teeth, I grabbed the blanket and pulled it over us. Not only would it keep us warm, but it would save my mate from potential embarrassment if he woke in human form and found himself naked. Closing my eyes, I let go of the stress of the night and allowed his sweet fragrance to lull me to sleep.

As I slowly began to wake, I felt more rested than I ever had in my life. My first urge was to stretch and flex my muscles, except then I would have to open my eyes, and I wasn't sold on the idea of leaving this perfect cocoon just yet. Except I was also aware of two other things—my face warming from the sun streaming through the window and the overpowering sweet smell of... Mate.

My eyes popped open as last night came flooding back to me. As I remembered, a new awareness spread over me.

Someone was watching me. Obviously, it wasn't a danger since my stupid wolf was too busy preening and licking his paws, preparing himself for our mate. Idiot. Except... Maybe I was the idiot, if I was wasting time worrying about my wolf when I could be gazing at my mate.

A soft gasp vaguely registered as I rolled over and met a beautiful pair of big eyes, so blue they almost seemed violet. My brain noted the dark hair and creamy skin, the rosebud lips and pink cheeks caught in a blush. I wanted to take it all in, but I couldn't pull myself away from his gaze.

When he finally spoke, the whisper-soft voice startled me enough to finally remember to breathe.

"Are you my true mate or Prince Charming? You smell like my favorite things, but you look like a fairytale character."

As I processed what he was saying, my mouth curled into a smile. "Sweetheart, I'm no one's Prince Charming. Although we could call you Sleeping Beauty. This is the first I've seen you awake since I found you on the side of the road." We could probably be having more important conversations, but if this was my chance to meet him for the first time, I felt being a little silly was okay. Whether we wanted it or not, responsibility would always be waiting.

His breathy giggle warmed my chest. "Sleeping Beauty, huh? I'm sure I wasn't at all beautiful. In fact, I'm lucky you didn't think I was roadkill. But I don't want to think about my injuries right now. Let's get back to this 'prince versus true mate' issue. I know you're not Prince Philip, because he not only belongs to Sleeping Beauty, but also, your hair's dark, and he's a blond. But Prince Charming belongs to Snow White, and I have neither a fairy godmother nor evil stepsisters. And I'm definitely not coordinated enough to walk in glass slippers. Still, she can't have you because I think you're supposed to be mine."

"I don't know. I think Sleeping Beauty is a good name for you. Or maybe just... beauty." Smiling, I reached my hand up, brushing my thumb over the soft pink, heart-shaped birthmark between his eyes. "You can call me whatever you want to because I am supposed to be yours, and yes, I am your true mate. I stopped to help you last night, and your scent nearly brought me to my knees. And now to wake up and find you're beautiful too... I feel like I've been truly blessed by the goddess. My name is Lucian Smith, but it's my prayer you'll choose to call me mate."

"Oh. *Oh, my*..." Scrunching his eyes shut, Thirteen shivered as he shook his head. When he opened them again, the violet orbs were glossy and filled with emotion. Blinking twice and then a third time, he stared at me for a long, poignant moment before carefully cradling his hand over my cheek. "That was the most romantic thing I've ever heard. It was even better than any movie or book. I only learned about true mates recently, and my friend told me they were rare. He was wrong, though, because I escaped last night, and here you are, the first person I met. I'm called Thirteen because we aren't allowed names."

I had questions. And slow-burning anger was churning in my gut, ready to avenge whoever had thought him unworthy of being named. Before I could ask anything, like who his friend was or who 'we' were, or better yet... where he'd come from, there was a swift knock on the door before it swung open.

Thirteen squeaked and burrowed under the blanket, which made me really aware of our mutual state of undress, since we'd slept in furskin. Fortunately, the blanket still covered me, and none of our parts had touched beneath it, so I knew I hadn't made him uncomfortable. I glanced at the door in time for Eli and Matt to walk in.

Eli's friendly smile and chipper voice quickly had Thirteen lowering the blanket enough to peek out. "Hi, there! I'm Eli, and this is Matt. We're the Alpha pair here in Lucerne Valley. I'm so sorry to barge in, but our healer told me you were awake and suggested I come help you bathe so we can enjoy breakfast downstairs. Isaac said he peeked in earlier, and you were completely healed after last night's treatment and a chance to sleep. But now, your body needs to eat. Goodness, why am I still talking?" Eli glared at Matt, playfully elbowing him in the side. "Why didn't you stop me? You know I get chatty when I'm excited."

Holding up his hand, Matt slowly shook his head, quietly saying he was having no part of anything. "How about I toss your clothes over, Luci? We can give our omegas some privacy and meet them downstairs."

I started to ask Thirteen what he wanted when I heard his voice in my head. *"It's okay. You can go. Eli looks like someone I will be friends with."* My mouth fell open in shock, but I had no doubt he was speaking to me. As if reading my mind, Thirteen giggled and did it again. *"Yes, I'm really talking inside your head. This is my secret superpower, so don't tell anyone. I don't know if every omega has them, but the ones I know... Never mind. Not my story to tell."*

Taking a chance, I tested to see if it would work both ways. *"Can I talk to you too?"*

"You just did." The little imp winked, his bright eyes sparkling with humor.

"Okay. Well, I don't think this is a superpower. It's part of the mating bond from what I've heard. Even though I haven't officially claimed you yet, Isaac formed the beginnings of our

bond last night when healing you. He said your wolf needed my strength to help you pull through after your ordeal."

Lips pursed, Thirteen softly hummed as he considered my statement. *"Is the bond the connection I feel to you? Aside from the delicious way you smell like spicy hot cocoa and freshly fallen snow, I could feel you when I woke up today."*

"Yes. Sorry to ruin your superpower theory, but I'm afraid this is a 'you and me' thing."

He giggled again, lifting a finger to boop the tip of my nose. *"Except you're wrong there. This is my superpower, and I can talk to anyone mindspeaking once I find the right channel to reach them. I'm not sure how it works. I just know I can do it. It doesn't work over distances—at least, I haven't figured out how. Maybe I can learn?"*

As it felt like he was mostly thinking and not asking a question, I simply lay there smiling, enjoying the sound of his voice in my head. Thirteen went silent, as we went back to gazing into each other's eyes. Or tried to, anyway. We were distracted by Eli laughing and Matt tossing my clothes against my chest.

Lifting my head, I bared my teeth at Matt, prepared to tell him to get the hell out. He didn't give me a chance, though. The rat bastard merely pointed at my clothes with a smirk. "I can read your mind, and no, you're not sending me away. Out of bed, Casanova. And don't you dare moon my mate, or I'll take a bite out of your ass. Hurry up about it, or did you miss the part where Isaac said Thirteen needs to eat?"

Thirteen sat up, holding the blanket to his chest as he gaped at Matt. "How did you know what I'm called? Do you have psychic superpowers?"

Eli sat at the foot of the bed, leaning toward Thirteen

with a conspiratorial smile. "No, alphas have the brawn. We omegas get the superpowers. Which I'm only admitting to because our mates are in the room, and I'm pretty sure the two of you were just speaking mind to mind. I'm guessing telepathy would be your power? No worries—your secret is safe here. Want to know mine?"

"Yes, please. Oooh! Are we becoming friends?" Thirteen was smiling so hard, his face was practically glowing as he sat there vibrating with excitement.

"Definitely. Any mate of Lucian is required to be my friend. We might as well get settled now." Eli winked, lowering his voice to a whisper. "My superpower is helping things grow. I can turn dead grass into something lush and green in no time flat. Maybe later I'll show you my garden. You won't believe how big my cantaloupes are, especially in this desert environment."

While the two of them chatted, I shimmied into my jeans beneath the blanket and climbed out of bed. After a quick, regretful goodbye for now, I left Thirteen in Eli's hands while Matt dragged me downstairs.

I waited until I had a cup of coffee in my hands before trusting myself to speak. "Is this where you give me your sage advice on how to be a good mate?"

"Shit, no." Matt sputtered with laughter, almost but not quite spraying me with his coffee. "The last thing I claim to be is a relationship expert. Anything I can tell you is common sense or what you'd do anyway. You know, have patience, be kind, yada yada yada. You don't know what he's been through yet, but we both know it wasn't normal. And since you're not only a patient guy but have more experience than me with charming lovers, I'm pretty sure you've got this."

Wrinkling my nose, I grimaced as I shook my head.

"Never say the word *lovers* to me again, Matt. That shit just ain't okay. Also, we might as well forget everyone I was with in the past since they ceased to exist the moment I found my mate."

Matt nodded with approval. "And your promise right there tells me everything I need to know. You and Thirteen will be fine."

FIVE

"THIRTEEN"

As we took our seats around the table, I prepared myself to tell my story over a breakfast of pancakes and bacon. So much bacon. If I could've, I would have stripped naked and rolled in the platter of bacon.

He must've caught me gaping because my new friend Eli grinned knowingly. "You're a bacon fan too, huh? The only thing I like better is a thick slab of ham, pan-fried and dripping with grease."

My hand automatically rubbed my stomach. "We get ham once a year, when Mistress delivers it on Christmas Day. But it's not greasy. It's actually thin shaved and kinda dry, if I'm being honest. Bacon was also a rare treat, but it's my favorite."

"A rare treat? What kind of meat did they feed you? Hot dogs and Spam?" Eli looked horrified on my behalf.

Shrugging, I shook my head. "We didn't eat a lot of meat. Master said meat is for alphas and regular wolves, not omegas. Our constitution is too delicate to enjoy it more often than as a rare treat."

Eli shuddered, holding a hand up as if begging me to

stop. "I don't know who this Master person is, but he is a big fat liar. Omegas aren't too dang delicate for anything. Please, I'd love to see an alpha push a baby out like we can. Heck, most of them wouldn't last the pregnancy, let alone the delivery. So now I have to ask, who is Master anyway?"

Okay, I guessed we were getting right into it. "I don't know, aside from the person who has always had complete control over my brothers' and my lives. He is mated to Mistress, but she only visits for two hours on Christmas Day and for half an hour on one of our birthdays."

Lucian and Matt were paying attention now. Matt was taking notes while Lucian started asking questions. "What do you mean by your brothers? And where did they visit you?"

"They aren't really my brothers, except they are because we grew up together in an old barn in the hills near the highway where Lucian found me. None of us know how. We were just... always there."

"How many brothers? I'm guessing they're still trapped, yeah?" Lucian looked worried for them, which proved what I already knew in my heart—I could trust this alpha.

"I'm guessing there were originally fifteen of us, but nobody knows One, and we barely remember Two. He was removed when we were little. My brother Twelve was taken seven birthdays ago, so I think we were about thirteen. There's barely a dozen of us now. I was about to be removed, so I had no choice but to take my chance to escape. Luckily, I'd made a friend on the outside, and he helped me get away. I promised my brothers I would be back with help, though. I'm afraid what might be happening to them now I'm gone."

Lucian and Matt both growled, then immediately apologized as if they thought I was scared. But that couldn't be further from the truth. Knowing these alphas cared enough to be angry about the situation made me feel safe.

After a moment, Matt drew my attention. Lucian was busy shredding a paper napkin and obviously working to contain his wolf. "If I might ask a question, Thirteen. What is it you mean when you say removed? I have a feeling I know, but it's best to ask."

"We never knew. Like I said, Two is barely a blip in our memory, but Twelve was our brother. He was there one day and gone the next. Master came and took him away. When we asked Teacher where he was going, we were told to mind our business. But then a couple days ago, Teacher took me aside and told me I would be leaving on Monday. Master would be taking me to an auction where wealthy alphas would bid on the right to be my mate. I didn't care to be sold like cattle, as my friend Alex put it, so I escaped, and now I'm here."

My mate stood so fast, his chair went flying. Running his hands through his hair, he tugged at the tips and growled, pacing. I wasn't sure whether to jump up and comfort him or allow him some space.

Eli patted my hand. "Don't mind Luci—this is hard for him to hear. Why don't you tell us about this friend, Alex? How did you meet him? Were you allowed occasional trips to town?"

"Gracious, no. Teacher keeps us in line with strict rules, and the guardians are there to keep us from getting away. We get to leave the barn once a week, and only to spend an hour in the sun while we meditate. And once a month, we get to take a leisurely walk around the courtyard in furskin when the moon is full. Teacher says it's necessary so we don't shame our future alphas. Otherwise, we don't go outside, and we are not allowed contact with the outside world. Once a week, if we earn it, we get to watch a classic movie on the projector. Teacher says we need to understand how society works, but the modern world is too gauche."

"Seriously? You were raised in, like, a bubble. How are you supposed to know how to act if they don't let you learn popular culture? Or, you know, actually meet other people?" Eli sputtered indignantly, his face a mix of both pity and anger. I didn't mind the anger, but I wasn't sure I liked the pity.

"Don't worry. My brothers and I have always managed to rise above and find ways to be happy. And there are a lot of good classic movies and books." I didn't know why I felt defensive, except it was awkward to realize precisely how weird my upbringing had been.

Eli seemed to understand, though. He scooped a pile of bacon on my plate with a smile. "Sorry, I didn't mean to embarrass you. Eat more bacon. It will make you feel better. There's a reason I call it the candy of meats."

To mess with him, I tried to look as confused as possible. "What's candy?" When his eyes went wide in horror, I burst out laughing. "Sorry, I couldn't resist. Fear not, even barn-raised bubble boys get candy every once in a while."

Snorting, Eli pointed at the bacon again. "I knew I liked you. Now eat and explain how you made a friend when you couldn't leave the barn."

I tapped the side of my head. "Superpower, remember? Our gifts were the one thing Teacher and Master didn't seem to know about us. When they started coming in, my brothers and I hid them at first because we thought we were weird. Then we started finding out about each other's and talking and... Yeah. So we voted to keep the secret between us, unless Teacher or Master asked or forced us to tell. Mindspeaking is my gift. I don't know how to work it perfectly, and I didn't dare ask for help. I heard Alex last year sometime, so maybe about eight or nine months ago? You'll have to understand—we try not to keep an exact track of time in the barn. Days flow together anyway, so what's the point?"

Lucian stopped pacing, coming close enough to rest a hand on my shoulder. "And where is this Alex now? Where was he when I found you on the highway left for dead?"

Shaking my head, I was quick to come to my friend's defense, explaining what happened as fast as I could. "There was one more thing. He recognized Jones as one of his father's men. All this time, he was afraid to tell me why he lived so close. He said he thinks his father is Master. But I know Alex's intentions were pure, and I refuse to blame him for the sins of his father."

Matt nodded soberly. "I hear you. My father was no prize either. Rather than hold Alex responsible for things out of his control, I think we will be grateful for the part he played."

Lucian dropped to his knees beside me, wrapping his arms around my shoulders in a gentle hug. "And we will pray to the goddess Alex lived. In the meantime, I think we need to figure out where you were being held so we can get your brothers out of there. If it were me, and I was an evil prick who had so many omegas on my hands, I'd be planning to transport them." Leaning back, he searched my eyes with concern. "Tomorrow is Monday. You think they'll try to take them to the auction you were scheduled to be in? I don't want to alarm you, but we need to be proactive."

"I don't think so, Luci." Matt answered for me, thankfully, since I was too dumbstruck to respond. "With such a large group of omegas, they would want a special auction with enough bidders to compete. They might get rich, but they take major risks. Even asking the organizer if they can bring all those extra omegas at the last minute would be enough to spook them, I'd think. Granted, I don't know much about the auction circuit. But I've heard they set them up far in advance with everything planned to a tee. The humans don't approve of trafficking any more than we do. And the Supreme Council would fry their balls if they got caught."

Trying not to cry, I bit my lip and clung to Lucian's arm. "I just wish my psychic or intuitive brothers were here. Or I knew how to reach them from so far away. I tried when I woke up, but... Nothing. It was like the channel was out of tune."

Thankfully, Eli lightened the moment with a change of subject. "If you've never watched TV, how do you know about channels?"

"Duh. The people in the movies watch TV sometimes."

"You're funny, Thirteen. I hope you know you're my new best friend." Eli's cheerful smile faltered. "I'm sorry, I hate calling you by a number. You need a name. How come you never picked one?"

I was confused. "People can choose what to call themselves? Huh. I guess it never occurred to me. How would I even decide? How do people normally get their names?"

Eli's head tilted to the side. "Usually, their parents or whoever is taking care of them as a baby. As for picking one, think about your favorite books or movies, maybe even an author."

I could answer without hesitation. "My favorite author is Charles Dickens. Can I have his?"

Lucian's lip curled up on the left in a half grin, half smirk. "You can have anyone's name you want. Why not take his? He's dead. It's not like he's using it anymore."

Nodding in agreement, Eli had a question of his own. "Would you use both names? Or will you take Lucian's name after you're mated?"

I stared around the table with a befuddled expression. "Wouldn't it be confusing if we both got called Lucian?" When everyone gaped in shock, I couldn't help laughing. "I'm joking, people. Even sheltered kids like me get to have a sense of humor. As to the name, even I know better than to call myself Dickens. The nickname writes itself, no thank you. Charles is good, though. Charlie for short, maybe? Definitely not Chuck. Sounds like a pervert to me. I like the sound of Charlie Smith."

Eli bounced in his seat, happily clapping his hands. "I love it. You totally look like a Charlie. And for you to take Lucian's name, because how cool is it that you match?" He must have noted the confused expression on my face because he pulled the collar of his shirt aside to show me a pale pink scar on his chest. "Neither one of you have the mark of a sire's claim. Now you can claim each other and share a last name. Ooh! You totally should. After Lucian bites you, you should bite him back. Leave your tooth mark over his heart, show everyone who he belongs to now."

"Or maybe not." I laughed uncomfortably, still not completely sure what the X represented.

Taking my hand, Lucian quietly explained, holding his vest open to show me his own bare chest. "When a baby is born, their sire extends a claw and marks them with an X, claiming them as their child. No one but orphans and unwanted pups are left unmarked. Or stolen ones, if that's what happened in your case. We won't know until we investigate further."

I didn't need to know because it didn't matter. At least, not right now. At this moment, the only thing holding any importance was hugging my mate and letting him know I would always want him. Marking him with my bite wasn't too bad, thinking about it.

Lucian

After a pleasant family style meal with Matt and Eli, Charlie and I finally found ourselves alone in a nicely appointed guest room. A guest room, interestingly enough, on the opposite side of the wing from their family. Actually, I was alone at the moment. Charlie was in the bathroom.

Scrubbing my hands over my face, I puffed out a breath and tried to decide my next move. Charlie would be thrilled if I turned on the TV, I was pretty sure. Hell, teaching him to work the remote would probably fill our evening once he got the hang of channel surfing. My wolf wanted to claim what was ours, but I was on the fence.

I mean, I definitely wanted to take my adorable mate to bed. But for the first time in my life, I wasn't sure what to do with the man in my bedroom. Did he need time, or was I overthinking this? And while this was a horrible thing to consider, I had to remember Charlie wouldn't be truly safe until he'd been claimed. If I waited, I would have to constantly be on guard against any alphas who might try to steal him, like Matt's uncle had done with Eli—a repugnant fact of shifter culture, but it happened every day.

If we did it tonight, I wouldn't have to worry about having backup for the ride back home tomorrow. Another plus? We had privacy here. While large, my one-story sprawling manor had thinner walls and a pack I still didn't completely know. I'd met everyone, but I definitely hadn't had a chance to interact enough with everyone in the pack. With a little over a hundred members, I'd figured getting acquainted would happen with time.

So yeah, showing up with my mate fully bonded to me would be for the best. I hadn't been intent on claiming Charlie so soon, but if it happened? Well... we were far enough away from the family I wouldn't have to worry about damaging any young ears. Not that I was rushing, because I wasn't. Charlie had been through enough, and even though Isaac had given him a clean bill of health this afternoon, I couldn't forget the way he'd looked last night.

I might have done some questionable things in my day, and I definitely had a reputation for never going to bed alone. But not only was Charlie unquestionably a virgin, he'd nearly died less than twenty-four hours before.

Shit. The shower shut off. I was running out of time to make up my damn mind. It wasn't like me to be so wishy-washy. I'd always gone with the flow and followed my gut when I made decisive choices. So far, it had never led me wrong.

Why, then, was I so torn up about this one? I knew I was overthinking it, but I wanted to protect Charlie as badly as I wanted to lick every inch of his body before claiming him as mine. Smiling to myself, I rubbed my chest when my wolf howled his approval at my last thought. Down boy. This was one for the human to decide. Through my inner eye, I watched my wolf turn his back to me. He was clearly disappointed.

I didn't blame him. I was honestly a little disappointed in myself. Claiming thoughts aside, I hadn't even taken my shoes off. Charlie had been in the bathroom and taken a complete shower, while all I'd accomplished was wearing down the carpet through my pacing. Problem was, I wasn't sure whether to strip down and slide between the sheets or undress and kick back over the blankets with the remote in hand.

Fuck me. Overthinking was an exhausting task.

The bathroom door swung open and thankfully distracted me. Thinking wasn't even a possibility. Charlie peeked around the corner with a shy smile. When he caught my eye, he giggled and darted out of the steamy room bucknaked and obviously ready to play. When he ran at me fulltilt, I had no choice but to catch him by the waist and spin in a circle before lowering him for a kiss.

As soon as our lips touched, my entire body broke out in goosebumps. What Charlie lacked in finesse, he more than made up for in sheer passion. Wrapping his legs around my waist like a spider monkey, his hands clutched at my hair as he turned my head the way he wanted it and deepened our kiss, his tongue licking at my lips until I opened them to let him in.

"Why am I the only one naked? Was I supposed to remind you to take your clothes off while you waited for me?"

Goddess, but I loved the sound of his voice in my head. Since he was clinging to me like Velcro, I fumbled with my pants, shoving them down while I kicked off my shoes.

"Sorry, don't laugh, but I was out here agonizing about how far we were going to go tonight. I didn't want you to feel pressured or push you into doing anything you weren't ready for."

Wild giggles bounced through my head. *"Seriously? Why do you think I wanted to take a shower? Eli told me how to prepare myself for you. I'm squeaky clean from stem to stern or however that phrase goes. Eli said sex is the best thing ever with the right person. And who would ever be more right than my own true mate? Also, no offense or anything, but Eli made it sound like you would be a little more take-charge."*

That shocked me into speaking aloud. "Eli said so, huh? And here I had him pegged as being the angelic type. Now I'm wondering if I should've encouraged this friendship." I was joking, but Eli being so open about sex did surprise me. It probably shouldn't, but he had such an innocent face. But then again, in my experience, the good ones were always the wildest behind closed doors.

Charlie was enjoying this a little too much. "Like you had a choice. He's mated to your friend, of course you had to introduce us. And apparently you'll have to think later, since his advice encouraged me to move things along if you were waffling."

"So you're saying you want me to think with my cock, not my big-boy brain?"

Humming, Charlie pulled away from the kiss to nip at my lower lip before answering. "There are a lot of things I want you to do with your cock, but thinking isn't one of them. You're my Prince Charming, remember? You've awakened me from my slumber, or saved my life if you want to be technical, so now you have to whisk me off on your mighty steed and give me my happily ever after. In case you missed the metaphor, the mighty steed is your cock, and my happily ever after is all the orgasms Eli described while you and Matt were on the phone making plans for tomorrow."

Lowering him to the bed, I motioned for him to stay put while I finished removing my pants and laid my cut on the dresser. "Two things, remind me to send Eli a thank-you gift for giving you such a thorough lesson on what to expect. And, I can't say this strongly enough—can we never talk about Eli again when we're about to have sex?"

"As long as we really are going to have sex sometime in

the near future, sure." Charlie giggled, bouncing up and down as he clapped. He was such a charming mix of seductive innocence, I was glad to know he was almost twenty-one, or I might have felt dirty. Honestly, as he learned more about the modern world and changed with the knowledge, I hoped he never lost this adorable vibe of boyish innocence. It was so sweet; my heart melted with every cute thing he did.

Naturally, right as I was thinking so, Charlie got up on his knees and cocked his finger at me, his eyes glittering like a tiny vixen. "Come to bed, Prince Charming. Make me feel sexy and show me how to love on you."

Jumping onto the bed, I wrapped him in my arms and rolled us over a couple times on the king-size bed, coming to a stop with him stretched out over my chest. "I'm sorry, Sleeping Beauty. Did you say love on me or rub? Either one works because the magic comes from rubbing together."

"Really? Rubbing what together?" His eyes danced with mischief, as if I couldn't feel his hard dick pushing against my stomach. Sliding my hand up between us, I nudged my cock against his before taking them both in hand and beginning to stroke.

"We could rub together like this. Or you could kiss me again and let our lips do some rubbing. Oooh... I like your wiggle. There's another kind of rubbing, pushing your chest against mine. I know I'm not very hairy, but I'm also not completely smooth like you. Did my chest hair tickle when it rubbed your nipples?" I kept my voice low, loving the way he shivered with every suggestive thing I said. Pulling his head down, I kissed him thoroughly before rubbing my lips along his jaw and whispering in his ear. "I can rub my lips all over your body. You know what else I can rub you with? Let me show you."

I could already smell the slick forming, so it was no surprise when I slid my free hand down his crack to tease his hole. Charlie went stiff and grunted as he shot a load over my fingers. He tried to bury his face in my shoulder, his heated cheek pressed against my neck. But I wasn't having it.

"Don't be embarrassed. That was just the first one. Honestly, I'm impressed you lasted so long. You're young, and this is new to you. But guess what? Being young also means a fast recovery time. You'll be hard again in a few seconds, if you even get completely soft."

His voice was muffled against my neck. "You mean it? You're not being nice, are you?"

"If I were lying, you would feel it through our bond, even though it's incomplete and new. Also, think about it. You're a shifter—you would smell a lie. And if you don't know how to detect one by scent, I'll be happy to teach you. But no, I'm not lying. Honestly? It makes me happy to know I gave you pleasure."

The wave of emotion flooding over me would've brought me to my knees if I'd been standing. I wasn't sure if Charlie knew he was throwing it off, but it left me with zero doubts of his affection. It might not have been love yet, but it was the start. And for the first time in my life, I knew what it was like not only to feel tender warmth for another person, but to have it returned. Even though I knew I should expect it from my true mate, it was mind-blowing. With all the feelings rushing through me, I forgot about being playful and guided him back for another kiss.

As I poured every ounce of my passion into our connection, I slipped a finger inside him, preparing his body to take me. Charlie, as I'd promised, was completely hard before I worked my second finger in. Thanks to his slick, his slippery hole was easy for my fingers to tease. My initial plan had been for him to ride me, but now I wanted something more personal.

Rolling us over, I guided his long legs up to his chest and pressed my cock into position. I broke our kiss, then pecked his lips a few times before bracing myself on my forearms with his legs slung over them. Biting my lip, I gazed into his beautiful eyes while I slowly pushed into his body. Working my hips back and forth, I pushed in a little, then pulled back. Pushed in deeper, then pulled back. Charlie was already coming unraveled and digging his fingers into my shoulders and grabbing at my hair by the time I pushed in completely.

I wasn't in a hurry, so I kept it nice and slow, letting my hips make the promises I wanted to scream from a mountaintop. *I will love you forever. You are mine, and I am yours. Nobody will ever hurt you again. You are the tastiest morsel, and nobody else will ever hold a place in my heart. Only you, mate, only you.*

Through it all, my mate made the best sounds. Charlie's soft moans, gentle yet possessive growls, and startled gasps of pleasure were quickly becoming my favorite noises. Each one challenged me to bring him more pleasure, if simply to see what sound I would get next. By the time I was getting close, Charlie had already come a second time, and a third was on the horizon. When the base of my cock started tingling and expanding as my knot bulged and my laniary teeth dropped into place, I knew it was time to claim my mate.

My entire body was drenched in sweat, and I was on fire. My balls felt so tight I knew I couldn't last much longer. "Turn your head, beauty. I need to get close to the back of your neck with my bite."

"Do it, alpha." Voice strained with desire, he turned his head as far as he could, begging me to make him mine. My knot completely formed, locking us together. Rolling my hips, I ground against him as I came. First pressing a quick kiss to his cheek, I stretched my own neck to get as close to the nape as I could before letting my teeth pierce his flesh. When I bit down, Charlie gasped and shot cum between us. My own cock was still pulsing as I emptied my load inside him while our partial bond became iron-strong, linking us together so firmly we would never come untethered.

Pulling my teeth out, I licked the bite to heal it and lifted my head when I heard Charlie's voice in my mind again. *"I know it's not normal for the alpha to be bitten, but I meant it when I said I wanted you to be physically marked as well. I don't want you to go another moment in life with your bare chest if it makes people think you're unwanted or unloved. Now that you're mine forever, I want the whole world to know. If you're okay with it."* He went from assured to hesitant in no time flat.

With my hand cradling his cheek, I looked him in the eye with a smile, hoping I showed all the affection behind it. "You can bite me anytime, anywhere. My body belongs to you. Mark it up however you want. And, beauty? I will be proud to wear your mark. Never doubt it for a second."

Charlie beamed as he pushed against my shoulders to make me lift up. Laughing, I thought about my knot and slid my arms beneath him and rolled us over instead. "Let's do it like this, beauty. I think you'll find it more comfortable."

As soon as he moved, Charlie winced and quickly readjusted his body. Thank fuck because it hadn't felt very good on my end either. "I was taught about the knot, Eli reminded me to expect it, and I definitely enjoy the way it's filling me, but nobody warns you about the logistics, do they?"

"No, they really don't. But maybe stick to small movements so you're not tugging the tender skin around your hole or detach my cock from my balls. I'm not sure you could, but ouch... it almost felt like it for a second there."

Charlie's eyes widened. "I'm sorry. I'd never want to hurt you."

"It's okay, I promise. I didn't know to expect it, or I would've warned you. This part is new for me too. I've never knotted anyone before." As tacky as mentioning my former sex life to my mate was, I needed him to know I'd saved my knot only for him.

"Really, Lucian? But... you're an alpha." I smiled when he hesitated after the *but*, as if being an alpha meant I was a slave to my knot.

"I don't know what you were taught, but alphas are capable of controlling themselves. The ones who don't are assholes making excuses to be pigs."

Smiling, Charlie shook his head as he bent to press a kiss over my heart. "Thanks for clearing my confusion up, but I have no doubt as to whether you could control yourself. But yeah, I was taught the alpha knot inflates every time you orgasm. Teacher said it was nature's way of propagating the species."

"Don't know who this Teacher is, but he's an idiot. I've never felt the need to go around knocking up everything in sight, though I really don't want to talk about my past. Especially while we're stuck together. It's not exactly romantic."

"True, but it is honest, and honesty is always romantic. Plus, I don't care about your past since I know I'm your future."

"Beauty, you're not my future—you're my everything. I

saved my knot because I've always held out hope of finding my true mate. My knot and my heart are the two things I have never given away until tonight. And now, they both belong to you."

Charlie blinked a few times, then sniffled. "See? Totally romantic." He leaned forward to kiss me, lingering long enough to make it sweet before baring his teeth and moving back to my heart. When he bit me, fire shot straight from my heart to my balls, instantly bringing me to a second orgasm.

Pulling him back to my mouth, I kissed him with all the passion I felt while reaching out to him with my mind. "Don't you dare lick the wound to make it heal. By morning, it will scar, and I'll have your mark forever."

We kissed some more before I carefully rolled us onto our sides, gently arranging his legs with mine so my knot hurt neither of us. Charlie was already yawning, and I was ready for sleep myself. The lights were still on, which sucked, but we could deal with it until we either came unstuck or passed out. I figured it was a lesson learned for next time.

Yawning again, Charlie snuggled against my chest. I guessed he was too tired to talk because he reached out mentally again. *"Was Sleeping Beauty too much of a mouthful? I noticed you started shortening it."*

Huh. I must've done it without realizing. "I don't know, but didn't you say Prince Charming didn't belong to her anyway? Beauty fits, though, because you're beautiful inside and out."

"Such a charmer. I'm going to call you Charming. Because you're more handsome than a silly cartoon prince anyway, but mostly because you are. Charming."

SIX

LUCIAN

THE MOMENT we sat down to breakfast, Eli started laughing and reached out to high-five Charlie. "Good job! That bite mark on Luci's chest is exactly what I was hoping to see this morning."

I shook my head at Matt. "Talk to your mate, man. This is inappropriate breakfast convo, dude." Matt's eyes widened. "You think so? Shit. You should've been here last Thursday. Eli had to explain why it wasn't a good idea for Noah to run around saying his cock was hungry. And then were the questions about why it wasn't. So many questions. We're all about bad table conversations in this house."

"What? Why would my little guy say that? Whose ass needs kicking?" I was ready to kill, but Eli started laughing.

"Chill, Luci. We have chickens now and he thought the rooster was too skinny because the fat hens were eating all the food. Someone," he paused to shoot a chilled look at Matt, "thought it was funny to tell our six-year-old that roosters were also known as cocks."

Matt's right hand went up. "Lesson learned. I won't be repeating that mistake."

I looked around the otherwise empty dining area, as if it would offer a clue. "Where are the boys, anyway? I haven't seen them at all since we arrived."

Eli nodded glumly. "I know. We miss them so much when they're away, but they spent the weekend with a family in town who have sons their ages. Matt says it's good for them to be kids. And it is, but I miss them and it's hard not to go bug them."

Winking, I shot him a grin. "Glad Charlie and I were able to distract you then. I mean, I can't promise this much excitement every visit, but we'll see what we can do."

"Speak for yourself, charming." Charlie shuddered, shaking his head. "No more excitement, please. After we rescue my brothers, I'll have had quite enough, thank you."

We visited some more, and when it came time to leave, Charlie mentioned how he was reluctant to leave our special nest. Eli promised the guest room would always be open for us and reminded him we would be seeing them and the rest of my crew this evening. Finally, Charlie got excited about going to Tehachapi and meeting my pack. Our pack, now.

Charlie and Eli chattered away, making plans to stay in touch via the new phone we'd found beside Charlie's breakfast plate this morning. Eli had spent the times we weren't all talking on teaching Charlie how to text, while Matt and I firmed up plans for him to bring as many men as possible tonight. We'd ride at dusk with his deltas in the hills as wolves, backing us up and tracking Charlie's scent.

One way or another, we were finding those missing brothers and getting them out of there. And the only people I planned on dying were the captors, hopefully at my hands.

Until we hit the porch steps, Charlie hadn't noticed anything but Eli. He stopped mid-conversation to squeal and took off at a run, rushing over to my bike and inspecting it. "This is so cool, Lucian! When I ride in the sidecar, I'm going to look exactly like Cary Grant in *I Was A Male War Bride*. Golly, my brothers will be so jealous when they find out." He stopped and glared as if I were purposely depriving them of sharing his fun. "You have to promise to take each of them on a ride, charming. Especially Eight. He will lose his mind."

Chuckling, I helped him get his helmet on and into the sidecar. "You don't have to threaten me with those fierce glares, beauty. I will happily take your brothers on as many rides as they want, but first we have to rescue them."

"Right. And let's get going. We have to get home so we can start making plans for tonight. I just remembered, you said you're Alpha of the Tehachapi pack, aren't you? That's where we live? Alex told me to check for a friend there if we got separated. But then I almost died and... Yeah. Anyway, Ford Silvers. He knows Alex, so he might know where he lives."

While Charlie blithely dropped a fantastic clue, Matt and I shared a look. I nodded and got on the bike. "I'll search for Ford as soon as I get back, Matt. After I get a word with him, I'll give you a call. Hopefully, we can narrow down the location and get a better plan in place before tonight."

"I'm counting on it. Ride safe, my brother." Matt punched a fist against his heart while I did the same. Conversation finished, I fired up the beast and headed home. As we made the ride, I truly regretted not having a speaker system or even a Bluetooth for Charlie. Happiness pheromones poured off him. The faster I went, the more excited he got. The goddess had truly blessed me with a perfect mate.

When it finally occurred to me to speak to him telepathically, we were already rolling up in front of my house. Raul and his parents were sitting on the front porch, which didn't surprise me. They'd clearly been watching for us, so I was impressed when they visibly restrained themselves from rushing over. As we hit the porch steps, Charlie was holding my hand, still gushing about the ride and planning for me to teach him to drive.

Just like he had in Lucerne Valley, Charlie stopped mid-sentence, distracted by the Ramirez family. His eyes sparkled as he studied them, clearly happy to meet more new people. When Essie arched an eyebrow in my direction, only my poker face saved me from laughing at the not-so-subtle hint.

Essie spoke before I could, staring pointedly at my chest. "Alpha, that's a nice mark on your chest. Me gusta, now you can maybe start wearing shirts since you've nothing to prove, eh?"

Laughter bubbled from my chest as I winked at the fierce lady. "I'll look into that, Essie. Now Charlie, these are the three most important people you'll meet today. And I say this because they live in our house. This is Essie. She manages the household. Her mate Pedro handles the winery, but we'll save the tour for another day. And Raul is the pack's Beta, which basically makes him my right-hand man. After you, of course. Ramirez family, meet Charlie—your official Alpha Mate."

Shaking his head, Charlie gently corrected me. "It's okay, he can be your right-hand man. Eli says as Alpha Mate, it's my job to rule beside you. To handle the things you might not think about, like celebrating special days or arranging gifts for new parents. I'm sure there's a lot more to it, but Eli promised to help me while I figure it out."

Charlie paused and smacked a hand to his forehead.

"Look at me, being rude straight out the gate. You gave a nice introduction, and I totally ignored these lovely people." Shaking his head, Charlie dropped his hand and went to Essie first, greeting her with an expectant smile. "Forgive me. I'm Charlie, and I'm so happy to meet you."

Now that her attention was fully on Charlie, Essie gaped at him like she was seeing a ghost. Standing, she crossed herself. Then she came forward and brought both hands up to cradle his face, staring at his birthmark. "Raul told me the story of how our Alpha found you and how you'd been kept a prisoner for as long as you can remember. Tell me, mi hijo, do you know where you came from originally?"

Something in her tone, along with her wet eyes and the tension I both felt and smelled coming off her, brought me to full attention. "Essie, is there a reason you ask?"

"Sí, es muy importante. Creo que conozco a su familia." She rattled off some more Spanish, but I was lost. Essie muttered under her breath, then smiled at Charlie. "You will wait here. My Raul will go get Dave and Tina Silvers."

"Silvers?" Charlie went from patiently confused to interested. "Are they related to Ford Silvers? He might be able to help us find where I was kept. The friend who rescued me told me to go to Ford."

Essie crossed herself again. "Ay, Dios! Raul, hurry, mi hijo. I believe the fates are fixing what obviously went wrong so long ago."

"Um, Essie?" I walked over and took her hand while Raul rushed to the golf cart. "Care to share what's going on? My Spanish doesn't extend further than pleasantries and how to find a bathroom in Tijuana." Nervous anticipation thrummed in my veins; even my wolf was pacing. Once again, it felt like we were on the cusp of a major moment.

"I would rather let you see for yourself, Alpha. I don't want to get Charlie's hopes up, but... well, you'll see what I mean when the Silvers family arrives. While we wait, let's sit. I made fresh lemonade and sugar cookies for Charlie."

Charlie inspected the chair options before picking the swing at the end of the porch. From there, we'd be able to see everyone's face, as well as the best part of the view. He sat and patted the spot beside him. "Join me, charming. This looks like it needs to be our perfect spot, don't you think?"

I thought any spot he chose would be perfect if he was there, but kept my thoughts to myself. I figured I'd save the mushy stuff for when we were alone. Mostly. I couldn't help if my arm went around him as I sat or the foolish grin spreading over my face whenever we touched.

Essie fussed over us, serving us treats while Pedro nodded and smiled. So far I'd heard him say three words, and I was definitely keeping count.

Before too long, Raul was back, pulling up on his trusty golf cart with a family of four on board. They seemed mystified but wore friendly enough smiles. I supposed getting called to the Alpha manor in the middle of the day was probably disconcerting.

For his part, Raul appeared less confused now, like being with them had shown him whatever Essie had seen. As they came closer, I quickly figured it out for myself. It was hard not to when the man and both sons exactly resembled Charlie, while the mother had his distinct violet eyes. Part of me wished Essie had prepared us for the shock I knew Charlie was about to receive, and part of me was grateful for the quiet interlude.

Raul smiled brightly, falling easily into graciousness in what could so quickly become an awkward situation. "Dave and Tina Silvers, you already know our Alpha. He found his mate this weekend. This is..." He paused and ended with a question in his voice, "Charlie?"

Tina started to greet us, then got a good look at Charlie. She gasped and swooned. Dave barely managed to catch her before she hit the ground. Everything went crazy, Charlie asking who these people were while Dave and Essie fussed over Tina. Their sons talked over each other, asking Charlie where he'd come from and demanding to know what the hell was going on.

Their tone didn't work for me, so I bared my teeth with a light warning growl. The older one immediately bent his neck in submission to his Alpha, quieting. The younger one didn't submit, though he did shut up, glaring at me but silently.

Given his youth and teenage testosterone, not to mention his clear desire to protect his parents, I didn't mind. Thing was, I wouldn't allow any accusations to be leveled at my mate, no matter who they were or what might or might not be happening. But until I knew more, I made myself remain quiet while I watched and tried to get a sense of things.

Thinking clearly was a struggle, let alone getting a word in edgewise. A piercing whistle broke through the hubbub as Pedro uttered his fourth word... and tossed in a few more for good measure. "Silencio! When everybody speaks, nobody is listening. Now that Tina is awake, why don't you help her over to a chair near our Alpha, Dave? Boys, I will ask you to remain quiet while your parents and our Alpha figure out what this means."

For a man who rarely spoke, Pedro knew how to take control of the room. Clearly, he had skills beyond managing the winery. Nodding gratefully, I motioned for Pedro to sit. "Thank you, Pedro. Mr. and Mrs. Silvers, Charlie and I are as mystified as you, I think. My mate has no idea where he came from. Is he possibly related to your family?"

Softly crying, Tina clung to Dave's hand on the arm of her chair. She took a tissue Essie slipped her, dabbing at her eyes while Dave tried to explain. "You see our two sons. Ford is our oldest at twenty-two, and Colt here is our baby at seventeen. The thing is, we had a third son in between. Had he survived, he would've been twenty-one next month."

Gasping, Charlie clutched his chest. "I'm almost twenty-one, and my birthday is next month. On the thirteenth, which is ironic for reasons you don't know yet. I'm sorry to interrupt. Please tell me the rest."

Dave grimaced, lifting a hand to point at the stork-bite birthmark on his forehead, then pointing at the similar ones on Ford, Colt, and Charlie. "This runs in my family. And those unique eyes of yours, Charlie, that's Tina all over."

When Charlie started shaking, I quietly lifted him onto my lap, cradling him sideways so he could see everyone while absorbing comfort from my touch. After a moment of silence, I nodded to Dave. "And you think Charlie might be your lost son?"

"I don't know what to think." Puffing his cheeks out, Dave sputtered a loud breath of exasperation. "We had no reason to think he was missing. You have to understand, with no pack healer or doctor, we've always depended on traveling medical help. Back then, an obstetrician helped any packs in need. He and his nurse would come throughout the pregnancy and then stay with us for a few weeks leading up to the delivery."

"I see. And these people, they delivered each of your sons?" I felt like we were getting close to an answer, but we needed to dig.

Dave shook his head. "No, Dr. J delivered Ford and Jamison—our lost baby—but we never saw him again. I don't know if he'd moved on by the time Colt came around, but we couldn't find him. Which was fine with me because I didn't think Tina needed the reminder of our loss."

All this talk of loss but no direct answers was making me twitchy. "Dave, let me cut to the chase here. What happened to Jamison? I need to know details." I hated to be blunt, but beating around the bush wasn't going to get us anywhere.

This time, Tina spoke. "Jamison came two weeks early, during a bad storm. Dave was out of town, filling a supply order to a restaurant in Los Angeles because our regular driver had the flu. Alpha asked Dave to go, but I don't remember why."

"You're right. I'd forgotten why I was gone." Dave shrugged it off. "There weren't many of us with a Class A license back then. Since I was about to take a month leave to be with the new baby, and Jimbo had the flu, Alpha asked if I'd make the run to give the other guy a free weekend before things got crazy. Then a surprise storm hit, and the truck broke down on the side of the 15 outside of Los Angeles, so naturally, Tina went into labor. I fought like hell to get home, but it was over by the time I did."

Maintaining her white-knuckled grip on his hand, Tina slowly nodded along. "The labor was fast—all of mine were. But that time, there was no sound of a baby crying. Dr. J and the nurse took a quick look at my son, and she wrapped a blanket around him and went rushing out the door. When I asked what was wrong, Dr. J told me he'd been stillborn. It happened so fast, and then..." She paused to collect herself. "And then, they wouldn't let me see him. Dr. J told me the nurse would clean him and bring him back in, and I was to rest in the meantime."

Running my hand along Charlie's back, I didn't know if I was soothing him or myself, but we both needed it to make it through this awful story. "I see. So what happened next?"

"Dr. J delivered the afterbirth and bagged it, but she hadn't returned. He lifted the garbage bag filled with, you know, the mess from delivery. The last thing he said was he was going to take the garbage out and find what was holding the nurse up. He told me to close my eyes while I waited. The next thing I knew, I woke up to Dave gently shaking me and asking to see the baby. The doctor and nurse had left and took our son's remains with them. Can you believe they didn't even leave us a body to bury? How were we supposed to say goodbye?"

"The kindest parts of me, as always, wanted to think they were trying to spare Tina's feelings, save her from further pain. But dammit, we both deserved the right to mourn." Dave lifted his chin, his red-rimmed eyes filled with pain as he growled. "All these years, we had nothing to grieve over because they stole our son's body. And our only proof of his death was their word."

Tina gazed at Charlie again, her expression torn. She almost looked as if she was ready to take him home with her, while at the same time, wondering if he was everything he seemed. I couldn't blame her; I'd be afraid to trust as well.

After a few moments, she almost nervously asked her question. "First Mate, forgive me if I'm overstepping. But do you have any information leading us to Dr. J and his nurse? Maybe they could explain what's happening here and what happened so many years ago. If they took you away and later found you were alive but were afraid to return you, it's okay. We won't press charges in human court or kill them under wolven law. I need closure... I hope you can understand and aren't offended by my asking."

When the entire Silvers family stared expectantly at Charlie, every protective instinct in me came alive. Solely through sheer force of will was I able to keep my wolf at bay, let alone maintain a civil tone. Or... I tried. I empathized with their pain, but Charlie would always come first. Whether intentional or not, Tina's question had been rude.

"Tina, Charlie may not be insulted by your question, but I am on his behalf. You know why your son's birth date was ironic to my mate? Let me tell you. Not only has he lived his life in prison with a large group of others like him, before yesterday, he didn't have a name. They were numbered, whether by birthday or the order they were taken, I couldn't say. I'm guessing it was the latter, but whatever, doesn't matter. The point is Charlie named himself yesterday after his favorite author. An author, might I add, from the limited amount of approved reading material his captors permitted."

Their eyes widened, but I wasn't done yet. "Think about it. A simple blood test will solve this mystery, but there's an easier answer. Shift. Your wolf will know its own pup by scent, just as it does at birth. Understand me, though. Whether or not his original identity can be proven, Charlie has been through enough at the hands of those monsters without being asked to defend himself or provide any kind of answers to anybody."

"Alpha, please accept our apologies. Especially if you felt your mate was offended, whether or not he turns out to be our son. Tina and I are fated mates. I understand the connection you already share and the need to protect him." Dave's sincere tone went a long way toward calming me.

"Thank you, Dave. You'll forgive me if my wolf is a bit on edge. Not only are we newly mated, but we met when I saw what I thought was a stray dog on the side of the road Saturday night. Turned out it was a wolf, and you can see how the story ended. But it was scary, and he nearly died right as I found him. Never having had any blood relations of my own, I can't imagine the pain of losing, or thinking you lost, a child. And having a doppelganger of what your lost child might look like at this age turn up? I know that's damn shocking. However, it seems to me if you possibly found something you'd thought was lost, maybe it'd be better to spend your day celebrating his return than mourning for another second."

Tina seemed nervously hopeful, while Dave lifted a hand to his collar as if he were ready to strip on the spot and shift. Before he could go any further, I held up a hand.

"Before y'all start sniffing each other, I want to tell you one more thing and ask a question of Ford." Their son glanced up at the sound of his name, eager to help any way he could. "Ford, Charlie was able to escape his captors thanks to the help of a wolf named Alex. His friend told him you were buds, to come here and search for you if they were separated. Do you know who I'm talking about and, if so, where he lives?"

Ford did a double take. "Alex? Yeah, I've been hunting for him all weekend. He was supposed to show up at our pack run and said he was bringing a friend. His dad owns a bunch of property on the east side of 58, in those hills just outside of our mountains as you head toward Bakersfield. I've never actually been there, but I have a pretty good idea where it is. His dad is a control freak and won't let anyone on the property."

Bingo. Now we were getting somewhere. "And how did you meet Alex, if I might ask?"

"Xbox. We'd been playing together for a while before we figured out how close we were to each other. I don't remember how—it was one of those random conversations. Anyway, we met in town and hung out a few times. Not often because his dad keeps him on a short leash, and he's been saving up to get out of there."

"Can you sit down with Raul and find the place on Google Earth, do you think? If we can triangulate the location and get a look at the property, it'll be a big help." Glancing at Dave, I offered him an olive branch. "You want in? My buddies are coming to help me rescue eleven other omegas who were being held along with Charlie. I was already planning to ask the pack for volunteers since our Delta squad isn't ready for solo missions yet. We don't know what we're walking into, so every able-bodied man is welcome. We don't know his name, but I imagine you'll recognize the same man you knew as Dr. J. And if not, I'll be happy to let him live long enough to tell you anything he might know. But after, we're getting the innocents out of there and taking down anyone responsible."

Dave's eyes glittered with a quiet fury. "You can count me in, Alpha. If the man is there who stole my son, I want to help take him out. But even more, I would like to help save those other omegas. Obviously, their existence will need to be kept quiet so we don't have people trying to steal them all over again."

Smiling, I nodded as if deep in thought while I reached out to Charlie. *"What do you think? You want to shift and see if they smell like family to you? Or would you rather wait and get to know them better?"*

"No, it's okay. I think I'd rather get it over with, but

thanks for asking. I'm not mad at Tina for guarding her heart and not immediately jumping to the obvious conclusion. I think we know I'm the one who would've been named Jamison. Probably still could be, but Eli was right. I do look like a Charlie. Is it weird I'm happy to know where I came from and see my family, but I don't feel anything for them yet? I mean, nothing more than any other nice people I would meet. I'm sure my emotions will change, but at the moment, I just want to see my new home and take a nap with you. My head hurts after the emotional roller coaster I've been on the past few days. I'm sorry if I sound like a jerk."

"Not at all, beauty. You sound overwhelmed and in need of a break. So how about we get this sniff-and-show out of the way so we can get you one?"

Charlie kissed my cheek before standing and smiling politely. "I know it's probably weird for a shifter to be shy about nudity, but I was trained to wear a robe up until the moment of shifting and drape it over myself before shifting back. Keeping us chaste was one of our rules and probably why we had private rooms with strict warnings about never having anyone in to visit. Although, since our rooms were basically converted stalls inside an old barn, there really wasn't room to hang out anyway. Sorry, I chatter when I get nervous. My point is, I'm going to slip somewhere private to shift. I'll meet you back here in a few minutes."

Essie stood, opening the door to the house and beckoning for Charlie to join her. "Don't worry, sweetheart. We understand. And never apologize for modesty. I've shifted in front of people my whole life, and I still don't like it."

While they disappeared inside, I had a quick word with Dave and Tina. "I think we all know Charlie is going to be your lost son. I'm excited for your family to be reunited and to put right to such a horrible wrong. But if I can ask a difficult favor—give Charlie time to get to know you. He's had a hard life and an even harder time the past forty-eight hours. It might not be obvious, but he's exhausted, and I'm worried about him getting overcome. Especially when I don't have a choice about bringing him along tonight. He's determined, and I won't deny he deserves to be there."

"We understand, Alpha. And I appreciate your protectiveness when it comes to my son." Dave smiled, holding a hand out to shake. Right then, I knew things would work out. It might take time, but it would happen.

SEVEN

CHARLIE

Meeting my birth family as a wolf had gone so much more smoothly. We probably should've started out shifted. After my mother hugged me about a million times and even my father was crying, Lucian quietly suggested we take a break to rest and process, then meet here for dinner around five, which was a relief. It was probably ruder than anything, but I'd been too worn out. My birth brothers stayed to help Raul search for Alex's home, while Lucian took me to a beautiful bedroom where I'd finally been able to rest my aching head.

I still hadn't seen much of my new home; sightseeing would come later. When I woke up, I spent a fun afternoon with my new brothers, learning about technology. While I was too overwhelmed between worrying about my omega brothers and being newly mated to let myself revel in the discovery that they were, in fact, my kinfolk, I'd enjoyed spending time with Ford and Colt. While Colt was excited to introduce me to TV later, today had been about computers. And all the magical things my new phone could do Eli hadn't had time to show me. The world was definitely a lot different than I would've known from my little exposure.

Now I was back in my new favorite place, my special seat on Lucian's bike, while we retraced my steps from Saturday night. Other motorcycles rode with us—my mate's crew, as he'd introduced them. One was missing today, an alpha named Nick. Matt said something about the absent friend being underground, but I had no clue what he meant, merely pretended like I understood.

Mostly because I didn't have the energy to ask. With so much new information coming at me from every direction, I was done with questions for today. My sole focus tonight was to rescue my brothers. Tomorrow, I could start the arduous task of acquiring new knowledge again.

As Lucian left Highway 58 and headed toward a small town called Keene, I knew we weren't far now. Not because I remembered my blurry escape any better than I did yesterday, but Ford had shown me a bunch of maps and satellite images. To get to Alex's family property, we had to head toward Keene to get to the mountain road leading to their place.

The road we were looking for wouldn't take us all the way—Ford said it probably turned to dirt and gravel at some point—but it would get us close enough. Lucian had sent some of our pack members, the ones with cars who would help transport my brothers, out for dinner in a nearby restaurant. While he and his crew planned our mission, a dinner party came up as the least suspicious way to get a group of strange vehicles into a small town with presumably nosy residents.

I didn't know the ins and outs of the plan, merely the part I'd play. Which was pretty much making a connection with my brothers. Since I was the only one who could talk to them right now, Lucian said my role was vital. While they could've gone in hot, having information from inside the barn and a way to contact them was the better, safer way. I was fairly certain Lucian had been trying to convince himself more than anyone because he really didn't want me anywhere near that place. I couldn't blame him, but wild horses couldn't have kept me away.

"Beauty, can you reach them yet?" I startled at Lucian's voice in my head, having been too tense and lost in thought.

Wincing, I guiltily shook my head. *"Sorry, I haven't tried yet. Give me a sec."* Switching to more familiar, well-used channels, I tried calling out to each of my brothers... to find nothing but dead air. I tuned back in to Lucian. *"Nothing. I'll keep calling them every minute or so."*

"Sounds good, beauty. Tucker checked in. Nobody seems to be home at the main house. Doesn't matter. I'm still going to park off-property, and we'll go in as wolves. Remember the plan, stick with me where you can, and if I ask you to stay in a safe spot, remember I'm simply thinking of you."

His requests were fair, and I understood. Problem was, I was equally concerned about my brothers. I would do my best to keep my mate happy and respect his need to protect me, but I wasn't making any promises I couldn't keep. If my brothers needed me, I would go running. All our lives, we only had each other, and I couldn't change our bond just because I'd found my forever alpha.

Crossing my fingers, I responded as honestly as I could. *"I remember the plan, charming. And I'll do my best to stick to it."* There. No lies had been told.

Lucian's responding chuckle made me smile, even as it made me shiver. *"Nicely put, Alpha Mate. I'll remember your turn of phrase when it comes time to make official speeches and shit. My beauty is smoother than I could ever be."*

Grinning to myself, I considered his words a compliment and switched channels again, moving between each of my brothers and calling their names. Finally, Six responded.

"Thirteen? Thank the goddess you're alive. Don't tell me they found you."

"No, either my superpower has a limited range, or I need to practice using it over longer distances. Holy cow, I have so much to tell you. But news can wait. I'm here with my alpha and a bunch of wolves. We've come to rescue everyone. Do you know where the guardians are?"

"We're going back to the part where you have an alpha later. As for the guardians, proceed with caution. Everything has been crazy, and they have, like, triple the amount of guardians on patrol. Everything in here is on lockdown, too. Teacher and several of the housekeepers have been staying here around the clock. We are not allowed to leave our rooms, so I don't know how you want us to proceed."

"Thank you, brother. Stand by. I need to check in and update my alpha. I'll be right back." Six didn't need to worry. Lucian and his crew talked me through every possible contingency. I switched over to Lucian. "I made contact with Six. Looks like we need to go with plan C to get them out, and he says they've tripled the security."

"Thanks, beauty. Make sure your brothers know to wait until we give the signal. Nobody's dying tonight, and the only way they don't is for everything to go like clockwork. You're sure about this, yeah? They can handle the inside?"

"Definitely. We never tried before because we didn't have anywhere to go and zero clue how far we'd need to walk to start searching for help. Trust me, none of the plans and suggestions your crew tossed around earlier were new to me. Except for the details about the outside world, but the actual escape part? We've spent years fantasizing and tossing ideas *back and forth. Now, let's do this. My brothers have waited for their freedom long enough."*

Lucian chuckled again, which somehow made me feel as if he thought I was the most precious thing ever. *"You got it, boss. I'll connect with the team, and you do you. When I park, start undressing while you wait for me to come around and help you out. We're going to shift and hit the ground running, in case any of those so-called guardians have scented strange wolves on their territory. We need to move fast."*

"Understood. Be safe, charming. I just found you. I'm not ready to lose you yet."

"Ditto, beauty. In fact, that goes double for you."

Smiling, I reached out to Six again. *"Okay, I'm back. We're going with Operation Worst Case Scenario. I need to check in with our brothers and get everything coordinated. Everyone holds off until I give the go."* I hesitated before nervously asking the question burning on my mind. *"Does this plan... feel right to you?"*

When Six took a moment to respond, I was grateful for the pause because he'd taken time to assess his intuition. *"My gut says yes, so let's do it. Wolf or human form?"*

"Wolf. Your teeth and claws will give you a way to defend yourselves if necessary."

Everything sped up from there. Lucian turned onto a dirt road, only to pull off and park a few minutes later. My helmet was off in a flash and set to the side while I shimmied out of my clothes. When he came to help me out, Lucian was naked himself, though I didn't have even a second to appreciate the view.

As soon as my feet hit the ground, we both shifted and took off at a run. My smaller wolf ran proudly beside our large, pure white mate. Aside from cautioning me a few times, he stayed silent as we flew through the night, scrambling across the field and over hills until we reached the meeting point.

Lucian and a large, silver-and-black wolf—Matt—took charge over the wolves under their command. I hadn't done a headcount, but Matt had at least twenty deltas, while Lucian had a dozen or so of ours here.

From our vantage point, it was easy to watch and see how well-trained the team from Lucerne Valley was and why our pack needed their help. Lucian had explained a lot of this to me already, but with so much new information, I hadn't really understood.

Heck, I'd spent most of dinner nodding and smiling because I was having a hard time keeping up with all the conversations. Especially with Tina, my mom. She was so eager to love me, and I welcomed it, but I needed to take it slow. One thing I noticed about shifters who'd been allowed to live normally: they touched a lot. Tina and Dave were constantly brushing their hands against mine, hugging me, or, even more personal, rubbing their cheeks against mine after the hugs, as if their human side was letting their wolf mark me. Maybe if I'd met them first, it would've been easier. But being so newly mated, I craved Lucian's touch and wanted everyone else to give me space.

I was probably an awful person, but I couldn't help it. Nor would I change it. Lucian finding me when he did, the way he did, was like a sign from the goddess herself. Not only did she approve of us being fated, but maybe we were each other's reward for not simply surviving, but thriving, after our harsh beginnings. Like everything we'd been through was the prologue and now we were free to write our own happy ending. I liked that idea. Now we needed to make it through the adventure part of the book and move on to the parts my brother Five would call boring. Not me, though. I'd always been a fan of the drama-free chapters where everyone just did their thing.

Gunshots pulled me out of my head and drew my attention to the yard where I'd spent so many structured hours. As our deltas began their attack, Jones and another man were firing. The sound of more shots echoed through the night. I couldn't see the other guardians where they were hidden, merely reddish-orange flashes when they fired.

Several wolves were obviously hit, but so far, nobody was down. One of the flashes rose toward the sky the moment before a body tumbled down the hill, followed by a wolf who pounced to finish the job. As the opposite side realized wolves were behind them too, some came out of hiding, while others ran through rustling bushes, their guns poking out long enough to fire before they moved along.

My heart raced, torn between the thrill of watching my oppressors die and worry for the wolves working so hard on my behalf. Shameful or not, I savored the sight of Jones, attacked by three wolves at once. One swept his leg out from under him, while the other bit down on the gun, tearing it away along with the hand holding it. When the third wolf swiped its claws across his jugular, I wanted to cheer.

Lucian, clearly sensing my emotion, brushed up against me, his sexy chuckle rolling through my mind. *"Such a bloodthirsty little thing. Let me guess, he scared you the most? The one who shot your friend?"*

"Yes. How did you know? From my reaction or his metal leg? Doesn't matter. Nobody will ever have to worry about him trying to sneak into their bedchamber while they're sleeping, not ever again. He always found every excuse to get too close to us. When we were younger, he would slap and

kick us if no one was watching. As we got older, he got creepy. One time, he touched my butt and told Teacher I was a filthy liar when I complained. I got fifty lashes and spent the week alone in my room while I filled a notebook with the sentence, 'I shall not lie.' He was a horrible person, and I only wish I was closer so I could smell his blood. If I'm bad, I can live with it."

"Doesn't make you bad, beauty. Wanna hear something worse? I wish I was the one who killed him, now that I've heard this. But I can live with it. The gray-and-brown wolf who slashed his throat was my buddy Devon. Finding out he got to avenge someone who tried to hurt my mate will make him happy." He paused at the sound of a lone howl, before responding with one of his own. *"There's our sign. Tell your brothers to move."*

Since they already knew to listen for howls, they would be in motion. Rather than distract anyone playing an important part, I reached out to Nine.

"What's happening in there? Did you guys hear your cue to move?"

"Yes, of course. This is awesome, I wish you could see it. A housekeeper was mopping the great room area when we all ran out of our rooms as wolves. She's screaming and running in a circle while Three has the water from her bucket shooting straight up in the air and following her. No matter which way she moves, the water goes with her. Ten has anything not nailed down floating through the air and slamming against the walls and... holy crap! Four is more talented than we thought. Thirteen, Teacher just ran out of the room he's been staying in. Remember how the ghost looked when he pulled off his own head and held it beside him in The Canterville Ghost? *He's projecting that image, and it's chasing Teacher."*

"Man, I wish I could see. Herd them toward the door. You need them to unlock it and get it open before Eleven can do his thing."

"Don't worry, Teacher is already fumbling with the bolt. He wants out of here, and Housekeeper is right behind him, yelling for him to move faster. The rest of us are blocking them from moving back. For the first time ever, I think Teacher is afraid of us. And... Hold on." He went silent.

"Nine! You're freaking me out—what's happening?" When he didn't answer, and I saw flames licking along the eaves, my body went cold. Frantic, I tried again. *"Nine! What the heck is going on in there?"*

Thankfully, he finally answered, sounding completely terrified, which didn't make me feel any better. *"You should see someone coming out any second now, I hope, because it's getting smokier by the second. Eleven did his thing. He only meant to set that ugly portrait of Master on fire. But apparently, it had some sort of accelerant because there was a loud whoosh, and fire spread along the south wall. The entryway is holding for now because Three splashed all the water. It sprayed out around the door and the walls here. The wood is so old, it's catching fast in the rest of the place, and it's about to go up in flames. Oh, thank the goddess. Hold on. I am almost free. I need to concentrate and make sure everyone gets out."*

As he spoke, the door flew open, and Teacher ran out with, yes, a hologram of the black-and-white version of The Canterville Ghost at his heels. Housekeeper seemed more afraid of the fire than ghosts, because she ran through the image and shoved Teacher out of her way. My brothers poured out, nipping at their heels with barks and growls.

I tried to get into their heads to tell them to pull back and let the deltas take care of the pair, but nobody was answering. I wanted so badly to run down and join them, but not only had I made a promise to my mate I wouldn't leave his side, there wouldn't have been time. My brothers ignored the other wolves in the yard and closed a circle around the two of them.

Teacher shifted into a scrawny, gray wolf. Snarling at my brothers, he tried to push them back, but he wasn't any larger, and they had both numbers and years of frustration on their side. Housekeeper shifted into an equally unimpressive wolf, but she tried to fight her way free. Unfortunately, she chose the wrong brother to attack.

In a heartbeat, Five fluidly changed from a wolf into a massive tiger. His jaw caught her around the neck and broke it easily before tossing her aside. When he turned toward Teacher, the man shifted back, holding his hands out as if begging for mercy. Five and the rest of my brothers swarmed in, piling over Teacher as they attacked. Nobody went to stop them. In fact, every wolf who'd come to rescue them howled their appreciation.

I was about to ask Lucian if I could run down and get a bite in when he spoke in my head. *"I know you want to be there, beauty. But you did your part—this is theirs. I need you to stay here while Matt and I go down. I'm sure the dickhead is dead by now, but your brothers are too frenzied for anything but an Alpha command to stop them. I hate to leave you, but with so many feral wolves, I think it's going to take every Alpha present. They are way too close to the burning building and the fire is starting to spread. We need to get everyone out."*

I didn't like the word *feral*, but looking at them, it kinda fit. Two of my brothers were playing tug-of-war with a leg, while another pair played fetch with an arm. I closed my eyes, not wanting to see any more. I swear on everything holy, if I'd seen anyone swinging his head around, I would've puked. I understood, but... eww.

"Then why are you still talking? Go get them. I'll be fine here." To make him feel better, I scooted closer to the bushes and sat down on my haunches. I would be able to watch, but I'd be protected from view.

Lucian didn't make it halfway down the hill before a rope went around my neck and jerked tight, a stick pressing my neck to the ground. Without hesitation, I screamed Lucian's name, trying to look back at the familiar-scented man who'd managed to pull off a sneak attack. *"Lucian! Master is here! I don't know how he hid himself, but he has me, and I can't fight back."*

"Motherfucker's signed his death warrant, not that I wasn't already planning to kill him. Hold tight, beauty. I'm on my way back."

Thankfully, Master wasn't watching Lucian when he veered off, leaving Matt to meet the other alphas and handle things down below. I figured Lucian knew what he was doing, so I focused on staying alive long enough for him to arrive. Especially when I smelled gunpowder and didn't scent any fear. Master was obviously prepared to end this and thought he had time to get away.

"Shift back, runt. I want to talk to you." When I hesitated, wondering if changing was my best move, he must've thought the stick was holding me too hard because he loosened his grip, dropping it beside me. "There, now shift, and don't get sassy. The one with the gun is always in control. Didn't the idiot at least teach you as much before he let you escape?"

Flipping around, I snarled, prepared to attack, but he lifted the gun. Since I needed to stay alive, I decided to obey and shifted. The rope around my neck fell loose, and I realized he'd taken me down with a dogcatcher's tool. Before he could grab the stick again, I quickly removed the rope noose from my neck and tossed it to the ground. Merely because he had a gun and I had appropriate survival instincts, I wasn't going to revert to the submissive omega who cowered before Master. Those days were gone.

Lifting my chin, I looked him dead in the eye. "I want to talk to you too. I met my parents. Who knew we were separated by less than twenty miles for my entire life? My only question is—are you the mysterious Dr. J, or did he give me to you?"

Master smiled smugly, his lips curling in pride. "Dear boy, nobody gives away an omega. You were part of the master plan. I had one year to abduct as many of you as I could. I figured the money would leave me set for life. I'm not sure I would've risked taking one so close to home, except I never planned on keeping you. With so many hungry couples wanting to start a family, and omegas in such rare supply, I figured a black-market baby sale was the way to go. Who would've known I'd get five million for the first one? And that was twenty years ago. Think what I'd get now."

In books and movies when the bad guy wanted to spill his secrets in the crux moment, I always thought it was crazy, like he couldn't resist bragging. And yet, here we were. Not only was the bad guy bragging—he was helping me buy time. Playing for effect, I went with a wobbly, weak voice. "It was about a payday? I don't understand, Master. Why did you keep us, if we were worth so much money?"

"Simply put, a much larger payday. After I sold the first one, I found out how much more he would've been worth if I'd waited until he was a little older. At least potty-trained, if not school-age. So I invested my earnings into hiring staff and had my old barn remodeled to keep you all in. Thanks to the formation of the hills, nobody had a clue any of this was back here. The wife knew because she started out as my nurse. We retired after we collected our fifteenth pup."

"Is that why we don't have names? Were we called the order in which we were taken?"

Frowning, Master shook his head, looking annoyed at something he was remembering. "I learned the hard way about names, and you can thank the missus. I was fine with letting you have names, only would've personalized y'all for the buyers. But as soon as I let her start calling the second one Joshua, I ended up an omega short and with another mouth to feed at home. She insisted on the limited visits, said it wasn't okay for a kid not to at least have Christmas and birthdays. So we compromised. She didn't ask for any more of my stock, and I let her visit so long as the rest of you didn't get named."

"What about Twelve? He left young while the rest of us have stayed until, well, now."

"Twelve? Oh, yeah. I did have to let another one of you go, didn't I? He got auctioned to someone in Texas, if I recall. Had a bad year and needed to recoup some profits when the crops died during a drought while the state was fighting with us over water rights. Then the oldest boy got cancer, if you can believe it. Medical bills damn near killed me, but he survived. Take what you get when you go shopping for kids, I guess. Alex started it. The missus was depressed when she couldn't conceive. So I grabbed her a baby from a mother who already had seven pups. Probably helped her and the mate out, if I'm being honest. They had enough mouths to feed. Never would've expected it to be so easy. Only have to be in the right delivery room at the right time, is all."

When the leaves rustled in a nearby bush, his voice trailed off. We waited in pregnant silence to hear another sound, but a rush of wind blew through, rustling more leaves and branches. Master looked back at me, motioning with his gun for me to move. "Speaking of Alex, you're lucky he didn't die during your great escape. Oh, he denied having any part in it, but I can see in your eyes he was lying through his teeth, the way I thought. Swore he was out for a run, decided to break the rules and see why I'd always forbidden him and his brother from visiting this part of the property. What I can't figure is where the group of dogs came from. Don't know whose they were, don't know where they went, couldn't even find a hint of scent or so much as a pawprint. The only thing we discovered, when all was said and done, was you missing."

"I don't know what you mean. I've never met your son. I wouldn't recognize him if we met on the street. I got scared by the dogs and ran off. Then I got lost, and the Alpha from the pack I was born into saved me. It's almost like fate had a hand in it. I don't know anything else."

"Bullshit. Try again. As the saying goes, never kid a kidder. Now tell me the truth, and maybe I won't put a bullet in your head. But start moving. I have a secret bunker not too far from here. We'll hide out until the wolves are gone. Then I'll get you sold and move my family far away. But I'll miss the payday and shoot you before I'll let myself get caught, so don't try anything funny. Turn around and start walking. Hands up where I can see them."

I lifted my hands but didn't move. If he wanted to shove me in a secret bunker, he would have to do it forcefully. I figured the odds were good he wouldn't really shoot.

Master wasn't about to let me get away with it. Lowering his gun, he pointed at my dick instead. "Okay, you called my bluff. I'm not risking my payday. I daresay I can shoot you and get you in the bunker before either of those alphas get back up here, though. And funnily enough, it won't matter to the buyers if you're dickless. They just need a hole to fill and someone to carry their babies. Whether or not you get off won't ever be their problem. Your choice. You want to keep your tiny dick, or shall I get rid of it so you know I mean business? You have till the count of three to decide. One... Two..."

"Roll to the right, beauty."

A huge white wolf flew from the bushes behind him before he could finish. While I did what Lucian told me, Lucian took him to the ground. Master never saw him coming or had a chance to fire. Lucian simply clamped his teeth around Master's neck and snapped it, killing him instantly.

I jumped up, brushing leaves from my body. As he rose, Lucian turned and shifted. We ran into each other's arms for a grateful embrace. I didn't even realize how scared I'd been until my heart stopped pounding. Lucian lifted me into his arms and cradled me as he began walking.

"Where are we going, charming?"

"Home, beauty. Home."

"Don't we still have things to do? I'm sure people need us, right?"

Cuddling me closer, Lucian pressed a kiss against my brow. "One of the perks of being in charge. The mission is done, and we get to leave because we can trust our guys to take it from here. Your brothers will be brought to our place, remember? So how about we go back and get ready to meet them?"

"I like your plan. Besides, Essie might appreciate

another hand. I know Eli, Colt, and Tina were going to help, but they might need me."

"Maybe. Probably not as much as I do, though. Now see, I was thinking we could get back early and slip off to our room. It'll be a great time to teach you how to celebrate being alive, especially after cheating death."

Smiling at the arousal I was scenting, I liked his suggestion more and more. I'd never heard of a sexual connotation for the word *celebrate*, but I was ready to learn any lesson Lucian wanted to give me.

EIGHT

LUCIAN

The day after the rescue, my buddies had already gone back home, and I was left with eleven new omegas to protect.

Essie was in her element with so many lost boys to mother. Seeing her in action, I knew she'd been right the first day. Sooner or later, I was going to have to call her Mamá. Just like I knew we would both eventually start calling Tina Mom.

Sitting in my newly assigned spot on the front porch, I was watching for Ash while the boys lounged around the porch, some in chairs, some on the floor. One of them even sat on the railing with his back against the post.

They were talking and giggling, sharing everything that happened while they were apart. Almost everything. Thankfully, Charlie didn't tell them the finer points of our mating. At least not in front of me.

As their laughter washed over me, it chilled me to think how easily they could've been lost, auctioned to the highest bidder as though they weren't people who mattered. Though it warmed my heart to see them embracing freedom, I hated to think how they'd been stolen directly from the wombs of their carriers.

Which was why Ash was coming today. Something this big was over my head, and we needed to do our best to find their families, if possible. I looked up at the sound of my name and Charlie tugging at my pant leg. He was sitting on the floor beside me, showing his phone to the redheaded one, who was apparently gifted in starting fires. Talk about having a superpower.

When he had my attention, Charlie beamed the adorable, nose-crinkling smile I noticed he gave when deep in thought. "What do you think, Lucian? Phoenix is the perfect name for Eleven. He doesn't believe me it's a name, even though it's here on the website."

"Yup. It is, all right, both for people and cities. If you ask me, a firestarter naming himself after a mythological bird who can go up in flames is too amusing to pass up. Not everyone has to take their name from books like Charlie and your other brothers."

Tom, the one formerly known as Fifteen, shot finger guns at me, then blew on his fingertips and mimed holstering them. "Only Charlie used an author's name. I chose an interesting character, so obviously I'm cooler than your mate. Sorry not sorry."

It was hard not to laugh. Colt and Ford had spent the night and half of the morning hanging out with their brother and his, well, other brothers. I'd encouraged it, thinking hanging out with guys their age would help them. And at the same time, seeing how tightly knit the little omega pack was would be good for the Silvers boys. Colt had already had an effect on everyone, and they were soaking up his lingo like dry sponges.

"What about me? I'm interesting, too, if you are. I mean,

Tom and Sawyer, we go together exactly like we did when we were Fourteen and Fifteen."

Tom shook his head. "First, it's not interesting when you copied me. I said naming yourself after the same character was boring when you chose it, and I stand by it. Also, you can't compare it to our former names because Sawyer comes after Tom, which doesn't work with the numbers."

"Whatever." Sawyer wasn't buying it. He cracked me up, this saucy little blond who had enough freckles sprinkled over his nose and cheeks to rival the fictional character he and Tom obviously loved so much. "Like Mamá Essie said, it's okay for us to share the same favorites. The same way a lot of people like the same colors."

Darcy, probably Charlie's favorite even if he never admitted it, was previously known as Six. He glanced up from the magazine he was flipping through to come to Sawyer's defense. "Be nice, Tom. We don't know where we're going to end up, anyway. There might come a day when knowing someone out there has the other half of your name will make you smile. And hopefully, you'll pick up a phone and call Sawyer and apologize for being an idiot."

Tom smirked, dismissively waving a hand. "Like I'm supposed to take you seriously when you named yourself after a total jerk in a Victorian romance novel."

Eight, now known as Romeo, started giggling. "I knew you didn't like *Pride and Prejudice*, Tom. You don't get the subtleties, that's all. Mr. Darcy is a beautiful, complex man. He's lucky he thought of it first and how I'm also a fan of Shakespeare."

I interrupted with my own two cents. "If you think Mr. Darcy is hot in the book, I'll have to introduce you to my favorite movie version. When you see Colin Firth's wet shirt scene in the lake, you'll never think of Mr. Darcy the same way again. Seriously, cinematic magic. An artist even made a twelve-foot sculpture to commemorate it. Look it up on your phone, Charlie, and then we'll start watching the movie. I say start because it's a miniseries with six episodes, if I remember correctly."

"Sounds like my kind of movie." Ishmael, the tiny brunette perched on the rail, was obviously ready to get started now. I hadn't got the reference of his name. Apparently, it came from some Melville book, whatever that meant. I wasn't an idiot, but I clearly wasn't as well read as these guys.

Five lifted a hand, as if wanting permission to speak. "Can we get back to me, Seven, and Three? We still haven't figured out names."

Charlie looked his way with a slight frown. "I already told you, go with Christopher or Robin. Pick one or the other, but as much as you've always loved A.A. Milne, it's perfect for you."

Humming thoughtfully, I studied the pale boy with the big brown eyes and light brown hair. "I think I have to back Charlie on this one, Five. I don't know how he appeared in the book illustrations. But the cartoon version, you're definitely a match."

Five giggled. "I know exactly what you're talking about. Teacher used to let us watch cartoons when we were little. But I want something unique like Phoenix. You think Robin is okay? When we were talking about it earlier, Colt said it was a girl's name."

"Any name can be a girl or boy name, if you want it to be. Are there girls named Robin? Sure. As proven by Winnie the fucking Pooh, there are also boys with the name.

If you like it, name yourself Robin and screw anyone who doesn't approve. No offense, but Cary's also widely considered a girl's name."

Cary, formerly Four, gasped with outrage. "How is that possible? Do modern people not have eyes? Cary Grant was the sexiest man ever born. I'll fight anyone who tells me I have a girl's name. Then I'll tie them up and make them watch a Cary Grant marathon with me until they admit Cary was the manliest man ever, and I'm the only one sexy enough to share his name."

"Cary is right, and so is Lucian. I'm man enough to claim any name I want, and I'll shift into a gorilla and punch anyone who says it sounds girly." Sitting up a little straighter, Five smiled proudly. "From now on, my name is officially Robin. Three, let's pick one for you now."

One of the more outgoing ones, Seven, looked around with a cocky grin. "I know my name choice. It's Paul. As in Apollo, the literal sun god. Get it? Because I can manipulate light like I'm a god myself."

Three high-fived Seven, then turned and whispered in Robin's ear. When Robin nodded, Three turned to Charlie. "Find me a water name, since controlling it is my superpower."

Knowing it would make them all break into shocked giggles, I leaned forward with a loudly whispered comment. "Controlling it? I think you meant to say you make water your bitch. Find him a powerful name, Charlie. Something strong to match his gift."

After he was done laughing, Charlie started offering suggestions from the app. He stopped in the middle of the list with a gasp. "Three, what do you think of the name Kano? It says here it's the name of an African water god."

"Kano..." He said it as if testing it on his tongue. "Yes, I like it. I'm totally the water god around here, making water my bitch everywhere I go." Rocking his head from side to side, Kano had us laughing as a vehicle pulled up.

When I saw Ash had finally arrived, I stood and waved him over. He got out and headed our way. I'd already given him my intel. Hopefully, he had some answers. I weaved through the guys, holding a hand out to Ash as he stepped on the porch.

After we shook, I waved my hand to encompass the group. "Ash Woodlawn, feast your eyes on the largest group of stolen omegas I hope either one of us ever comes across. Gentlemen, this is the Territory Chief of California. He oversees all the packs and is the guy most likely to help us find your kin, if possible."

Charlie came up beside me, earning his own introduction. "Ash, this is my mate, Charlie."

Ash took Charlie's outstretched hand, but rather than shake it, he lifted it and kissed my mate's knuckles. With anyone else, I might've had a problem. But with Ash, I figured it was simply old-school courtliness. Plus, Charlie deserved to feel special.

"It's a pleasure to meet you, Charlie. You were very brave, son." When Charlie looked confused at Ash calling him *son*, I made a mental note to explain later. Charlie hooked his arm through Ash's, acting every bit the Alpha Mate as he walked Ash around the porch, introducing him one by one to his brothers.

I made my way back to my seat and waited for Ash and Charlie to make the rounds. When they were done, Charlie offered Ash a seat to my right and excused himself to find Essie and see about refreshments. Ash watched Charlie slip inside before turning to me with a shake of his head. "You found a good one there, Lucian. Congratulations, son. I wish both of you a lifetime of nothing but happiness and zero drama from here on out. I think you've both had your share, don't you?"

"Ash, you're preaching to the choir. So let me leave it at amen and from your lips to God's ears. Or the goddess's, in our case." We both chuckled, knowing it was true. Charlie returned a moment later, announcing Essie would be out in a few with lemonade and cookies. Smiling to myself, I wondered if she had a lot left over from yesterday or if it was her go-to.

We made polite small talk for a few minutes before Ash got down to business. "Needless to say, only my assistant knows about the guys right now. I'm guessing your pack knows not to talk, yeah?"

Nodding somberly, I pursed my lips, not wanting to think about what might happen if word got out about my pack hosting eleven mature omegas. "No worries, Ash. I saw what went down when my pack's former Alpha and his buddies found out about Eli's little brothers. If they would risk their lives for children, I don't want to think what might happen if people knew about these guys."

Ash looked as irritated as I felt at the mention of what had gone down in Lucerne Valley. "Eventually, I'll need to report this to the Supreme Council, but I'm hoping to get these guys back to their home packs before I do. Paperwork can be a real bitch, you know? Funny how long it takes for reports to get typed and emails to be sent."

"Funny indeed, isn't it?" I winked, appreciating what he was doing to delay the inevitable. "In the meantime, they'll be safe here with me to protect them. Matt loaned me some deltas. With them here watching my borders and teaching mine how to do it when they leave, I feel like this might be the perfect place for them right now anyway. Our geography creates a natural barrier, and we're so small. I don't think we're even on the radar of most of the other packs."

"No, not at all. I think most of them have forgotten there's even a pack located in these mountains. If I was a religious man, I might think the goddess had her hand in this one. But since I'm a man of science, I'll merely say sometimes things work out the way they're meant to."

Personally, I thought Ash might be a little more religious than he wanted people knowing, but I let the question pass and moved the conversation along. "What did you find out about this Dr. J, if anything? Charlie is worried about the doctor's son, the one who helped him escape. Not only was Alex shot Saturday night, but the asshat stole him as well. I've had eyes on the place, but so far, the family hasn't returned. The sole reason we know Alex survived is because the douche canoe said as much to my mate."

Charlie was already sitting beside me, but he curled in closer, as if afraid to hear bad news. I ran a hand along his back and smiled at his brothers, who were watching nervously while Ash told us what he knew.

"We haven't found the family, yet. The property is listed under the name of a Dr. Egbert Jenkins. I looked him up, and the mate we have on record is a Linda Jenkins. They're also legally married, not that it matters to us. As for children, they never reported any births, so my office doesn't have a record of their boys. I reached out to some of our people in law enforcement. They are watching the family bank account and credit cards. But I'll tell you her car was found in long-term parking at LAX, so she could be anywhere right now."

"Fuck, and she's got the boys with her. And neither one

of them knows she's their abductor, rather than their mother. Well, at least we have names. What are we going to do with these brothers? How are you going to find their families while keeping it a secret?"

Ash smiled apologetically at the guys. "Hate to say it, but I need to take a DNA sample from each of you. I know it sounds invasive, but all you have to do is swab the inside of your cheek with the kit I'll give you and then write your name on it."

"And what will a paternity test accomplish, Ash? Aside from proving who their kinfolk are, when you find them, anyway."

"Exactly, Lucian. With the DNA in place, the families will have to prove themselves while your guys stay safely here until we find matches. My assistant is going through the records as we speak, looking for reported stillbirths in the territory from twenty to twenty-one years ago. After that, if we haven't found matches, I'll reach out to every pack alpha in the state and pick brains. Losing a child is a hard thing. Some people never get over the grief. It won't surprise me if every stillborn pup wasn't even reported. But it's a starting point."

Charlie beamed at Ash. "Not only is it a starting point, it shows you care enough to think it through. Thank you for your help, sir. And if you could, please don't stop searching for Alex. He saved my life. I want to thank him and make sure he's okay."

"This Alex kid, he was really your friend?" Ash didn't have the particulars. We couldn't share them without talking about the omega's special powers.

"Yes, sir. I refuse to believe otherwise. Besides, why else would he get shot helping me escape?"

Laughing so hard he began to cough, Ash had to stop

and pounded a fist against his chest. "Charlie, you'd be amazed what some guys would do for a pretty face."

Charlie turned and batted his lashes at me. "Your friend was talking, but all I heard was 'pretty face.'" Luckily, Essie came out with refreshments and distracted us from any more heavy conversation.

NINE

CHARLIE

Three weeks later...

Fortunately, nobody but my brothers was around when Romeo brushed my hand as we both reached for a slice of bacon. Otherwise, I might have been annoyed when he accidentally discovered the secret I'd been suspecting, or part of it anyway.

"Charlie! When were you going to tell us about the baby? After I was gone? Sheesh! Do you guys know what you plan to name her yet?"

Propping my chin on my hand, I lazily chewed my bacon while my brothers pretty much lost their minds. Freaking Romeo, though. He usually knew better than to share things he saw without asking first. To be fair, he'd discovered a happy surprise.

Romeo looked my way and froze, then immediately hollered for everyone to stop talking. "Charlie, noooo... I did it again, didn't I? I'm so sorry. I got caught up in the moment and didn't even think. And even if you knew about the pregnancy, how would you know the gender yet? Me and my big mouth. If it helps, I totally feel like crap now."

"Good, it serves you right." I stuck my tongue out, then passed him a piece of bacon. "Don't worry about it. Anyone would goof if they accidentally discovered something exciting."

"So exciting." Bobbing his head, Romeo's smile proved he was genuinely thrilled. "You're the first of us to find your true mate, and now you'll be the first to have a baby. I saw a picture of her in my head, Charlie. And it was clear as day. She was older, school-aged, I would say. And so pretty. A miniature version of your mother but with Lucian's nose. I don't envy you because she looked smart, too. Like she'll be quite the handful."

I covered my mouth with both hands while I blinked away tears. When blinking didn't work, I tried fanning my face. "Doggonit, Romeo. Don't you know better than to make a pregnant person cry? I can picture her now, and I have to wait forever to meet her."

Phoenix snorted, rolling his eyes. "Not sure when four months became forever, unless Teacher taught you a special biology course the rest of us missed."

Pushing his chair back, Darcy jumped up and ran around to hug me. "Ignore Phoenix. The rest of us do. Four months feels like forever to me now too. Your daughter sounds delightful, and I feel like Romeo is right. She's going to be smart and keep you on your toes. Don't worry. No matter where we are, you'll always have us to support you."

Frowning, Paul looked at the clock hanging on the wall behind the table. "What time is Ash coming, anyway? Did Lucian say?"

The reminder six of my brothers were leaving today didn't help my fight against the impending tears. Sniffling, I reached for my napkin. "High noon. I can't believe you guys forgot. It's so fitting. Except Ash is no Gary Cooper. And he's not coming to try to seek revenge by killing me."

Darcy got what I meant. "No, but I see the correlation. He isn't coming to take your life, just half our brothers." Sighing softly, Darcy went back to his seat and took a sip of tea. "It's going to be okay, though. I would tell you guys if it wasn't. My intuition is clear—this is going to be a good thing for those of you who are leaving today."

Nodding his agreement, Romeo looked around the table. "That's why I made a point of touching each of you today. Charlie was an accident, but the rest of you were on purpose. I'm sorry I'm leaving and won't be here when the rest of your families are found, but I'm nothing but a phone call away."

Cary snorted, twirling his pointer finger at the ceiling. "Whoop-de-doo, Romeo. No offense, but your psychic powers only work by touching someone. You might be able to cheer us on by phone, but you won't be able to touch us and get a vision. What if the rest of us belong to serial killers or bank robbers? What if my parents turn out to be both deaf and blind? They would never be able to understand my superpowers if I can't project images or distort sound for them."

When we all started laughing at Cary's ridiculousness, he sniffed and held up his hands. "What? It could happen. Obviously. I mean, look at Alex and Josh. I bet they never thought their parents were kidnappers, now did they? Or how Josh started his life named Two and living in a barn with fourteen other stolen babies."

Harvey sent a glass of water flying through the air, hovering over Cary's head. "Quit trying to freak everyone out or I'm going to dump this on you. Don't test me. You know I'll do it."

With a wink to Harvey, I grinned at Cary. "Don't risk it. He's the crazy one. Who else would name themselves after an imaginary friend?"

Harvey didn't buy my playful wink for a second. Instead, he lifted another glass to float over my head. "Et tu, Brute? We don't joke about Jimmy Stewart movies, remember? Besides, going with Harvey was my inside joke about my powers. If people ever suspect I'm telepathic, I'll claim I have a ghost as a friend."

"Let me guess, and your friend would be a six-foot-three rabbit like Harvey?" Even though I was teasing, I thought Harvey was the perfect name for my telekinetic brother. Also, I still wasn't sure whether the invisible rabbit in the movie was real or not. Either Jimmy Stewart's character was deeper than he seemed at face value, or there really was a rabbit somewhere in there. Frankly, the whole thing gave me the creeps, but Harvey liked it, and nothing else mattered.

"I don't know. Maybe I'll get Cary to come visit and trot out the Canterville Ghost again. His version was beyond epic."

As we started laughing at the memory, I tried not to think about the scarier aspects of our escape. And none of us had ever mentioned the way Teacher had died... or how my brothers had ripped his body apart. Lucian promised it was totally present and accounted for when they cleaned the scene, so at least no one went Donner Party on him. But then again, I couldn't imagine he would've had the best flavor, even if someone had cannibalistic tendencies. Someone so evil couldn't possibly taste like anything other than sulfur and cod liver oil.

Darcy got Romeo's attention once everything fell quiet. "When you were touching everyone, did you see a family or mates for all of us? I know you don't like to share the future. But... I have a feeling my parents won't be found. You don't have to tell me if you don't want to, but if you saw anything from my future, I wouldn't mind hearing. I promise it won't change any choices I make. You know I always follow my intuition."

After a second's hesitation, Romeo nodded. "You have a true mate, and you'll meet him through one of Lucian's friends. I won't tell you which one because it's not my place to hurry fate along. You'll find out when the time is right. But I think you're correct about your family because in the vision I saw, Lucian had a baby on his hip, and you were still living here."

"Makes sense, since Lucian promised to protect any of us who had nowhere else to go." Darcy stared off into the distance before looking back at Romeo and waggling his eyebrows. "So you saw my true mate, huh? Do I get a hint? Eye and hair color, maybe? Is he sexy? Wait, don't answer. Then I'll be angry because you said my mate is sexy, and I'll have to call and yell at you after I meet him."

Throwing my napkin at him, I snorted and shook my head at Darcy. "You're ridiculous, and we both know it. You can't get jealous over someone you haven't even met yet. At the moment, it's a potential future, nothing more, nothing less."

"Except my visions never lie." Romeo winked and shot a grin at Darcy. "Don't worry, he's not my type, but I think he is definitely yours. We all know how I feel about long hair on a man, right? While you seem to like it for some reason. When Lucian's friend shows up with a tall, lean man with long, honey-colored hair, I'll expect a phone call. And instead of yelling at me, you'll be telling me I'm an idiot for not calling him sexy. Maybe if you need to cut his hair, but nah. The fates have given him to you. He just doesn't know it yet."

Darcy stretched his hand over the table to take Romeo's. "I know you can't see your own future, which sucks. But let me return the favor. I feel like you're going to be happier than you've ever dreamed when you meet your family. And when I think of you and a true mate, I feel strongly you are also going to find one." Leaning back, Darcy looked around the table. "Honestly? I feel like each of us are going to find our true mates. And as I say it aloud, my gut tells me I'm correct."

There were those tears again. "Everyone said Lucian found me the way he did because the goddess was blessing me, wanting to make up for everything I'd been through in life. She doesn't care any less for any of you. If the goddess allowed me to find the mate the fates designed for me, I know she would do the same for any of you. And as Ash would say, you all know I'm not real religious. So if I believe in the possibility of a merciful goddess, maybe you can believe a true mate is coming your way. It might not be today or tomorrow, but he's coming. Or she. What do I know? But somebody is out there for every one of us, I know it."

While my brothers talked about the future and the possibility of finding their own true mates, I tried to ignore the clock. In my heart, I knew after Ash left with six of my brothers, the five of us who remained would miss them, and life would never be the same for any of us. Even though my own life was a dream come true, and I didn't begrudge any of them having the same, it was still going to be hard. But then again, change always was. At least this time, I would not only know where they were, but they'd each be a phone call and a visit away.

As I sipped my tea, a calm settled over me, and I slowly allowed myself to be at peace with my brothers' impending departure. Now if I could just figure out which one of Lucian's friends knew someone with long honey-colored hair without tipping Darcy off or tempting fate...

TEN

LUCIAN

If anything was hotter than having a wet dream about my own mate, it was waking from said dream to find the wet heat of his mouth surrounding my cock. His soft moan pulled my attention.

Charlie kneeled between my legs, thrusting his own dick into his hand while he bobbed up and down on mine.

"Fuck, beauty. You're sexy as hell right now."

And damned if he didn't hold my gaze while increasing his suction as he bobbed faster. His free hand cradled my balls, rubbing them with the slightly firm pressure I loved while his thumb stroked the base of my shaft.

I'd woken up at the perfect time because I was about to come hard. "Charlie... I'm gonna... You might want to..." I couldn't even finish a sentence. My thoughts were spiraling as my body came undone.

With a naughty wink just for me, Charlie went down all the way until his nose was buried in my thatch of hair, and my cock was pushing into his throat. His tongue stroked a prominent vein while his hand gave my balls the light squeeze I needed to push me over the edge.

As if his teasing wasn't enough, he shot his own load, filling my nostrils with the scent of his release. Lightning flooded my veins as my balls jerked, and my cock pulsed as I came. Charlie swallowed. His throat muscles convulsing and pressing around me pushed my orgasm to the next level, until I was lightheaded and clutching at the mattress, shouting his name.

My head was spinning when Charlie came up for air and crawled up my body, stretching over my chest for a kiss. Luckily, he was content to peck at my lips and trace his tongue around my open mouth while I caught my breath. As soon as my vision returned to normal, Charlie covered my mouth completely and brushed his cum-covered tongue against mine as he fed me what was left of what I'd given him.

Running my hand down his back, I cupped his ass, sitting up and pulling him onto my lap as I moved. We kissed a little longer before finally breaking away.

His eyes were filled with adoration as he smiled, cupping his hands around my face before moving in for another kiss. This time, he rubbed his lips against mine while he slowly pulled away. "I love you, Lucian. So much."

"Charlie, my little beauty. I love you too, more than anything in the world. If I've never said the words, my mistake for worrying it was too soon. Everything else happened so fast. I wanted you to know I'd given my love time to grow appropriately, and my affections weren't completely pheromone-based."

"Your explanation sounds so silly when you say it out loud, but… I was doing the same thing."

We shared a laugh. Then I studied him closer. "What happened to make you say the words today?" I didn't think it had anything to do with his sadness about so many of his brothers leaving yesterday, but maybe their departure made him remember all over again how fast life can change. Which was why I should've said the words already, dammit.

"Don't overthink it, Lucian. And don't start getting protective or trying to carry me everywhere when I tell you this, okay?"

Lifting a brow, I searched his gaze. "Beauty, don't ask me to make a promise when I don't know why. The only thing I can swear is to do my best to restrain my inner caveman, fair enough?"

His instant reactionary giggle never failed to warm my heart. "Works for me. So I was already suspicious because my stomach has felt weird the last few days, and I've noticed some foods haven't been smelling right. Those are minor signs, but I was watching for them because Eli warned me true mates usually conceive immediately. And then Romeo touched my hand and dropped the bomb in the middle of breakfast."

My head was spinning again, this time for a much more important reason than a mere orgasm. "Charlie, are you saying what I think you are?"

"Yes, we're having a baby. I'll have to visit the doctor in Eli's pack to know how far along I am, but yeah. And if you don't mind spoilers, Romeo told me what we're having."

Rocking my head from side to side, I took a moment to consider it. Did I want to know? And more importantly, could I handle not knowing when Charlie did? Not to mention I'd be asking him to keep a pretty big secret for the next few months. Or at least until the first ultrasound. Putting either of us through so much was silly. Especially when my beauty was probably dying to tell Eli, if he hadn't already. Hell, his brothers all knew, so why not?

As if reading my mind, Charlie smiled regretfully. "I'm

sorry my brothers found out before you. Romeo blurted it before he stopped to think. I hope you know you're the first person I'm officially telling. Heck, I even swore my brothers to secrecy. I planned to tell you last night while we were stargazing from our porch swing, but then my parents came over and stayed so long after dinner. We got caught up in conversation and missed our porch time."

Even though I knew it was true, I loved hearing him refer to our porch time. In the three and a half weeks we'd been together, sitting on the porch before bed had become our tradition. We'd cuddle on the swing and drink a hot beverage while watching the stars. It was the most peaceful and glorious moment of my day, and I looked forward to it the minute my eyes opened in the mornings.

"Don't worry. You're telling me now. And yes, I definitely want to know what we're having. I don't want to make you keep a secret. Plus, we both know how nosy I am."

My joke got me another giggle. Charlie moved to whisper in my ear. "Congratulations, charming. We're having a girl."

And easy as pie, I fell in love all over again. This time with a tiny little blob of cells, my daughter. A daughter. Holy shit.

Flipping him over onto his back, I blew raspberries against his stomach before pressing a wide circle of kisses around it. Charlie squealed and giggled the whole time, undoubtedly both from excitement and the way my whiskers tickled his tender flesh. When I sat up again, I bounced on my hands and knees beside him like an overgrown pup. "I can't believe we're having a little girl. That's amazing, beauty. You're going to have to watch me so I don't spoil her to death."

Charlie gave an evil laugh. "From what Romeo said, we

might want to be careful. He says she's going to be smart as anything and a total handful."

I jumped up and scooped him from the bed, cradling him against my chest as I spun in a circle before heading out of our room. "Of course she will be every bit of those things. With us as parents, we can't expect anything less. Our baby girl will be smart and beautiful. And probably spoiled. We should get used to the idea."

My voice traveled, preceding me into the breakfast nook, where Tina and Essie were gossiping over a cup of tea and poring through a recipe book. They both looked up with their mouths hanging open.

Tina pressed a hand to her heart, her lip trembling as she spoke. "Did I hear you right? Are you having a baby?"

Waving a hand, Essie nodded sagely. "Of course they are, dear. They are true mates, no? They probably conceived straight off the bat. Most do, from what I've heard."

"You're not wrong. I'd forgotten how fast I got pregnant with Ford." Tina seemed so happy, she was glowing.

I set Charlie down at the table and turned to get my coffee. At this point, when he officially shared our news, it felt anticlimactic. "Since you've worked it out between you, the answer is yes. Lucian and I are having a baby. And according to my brother who has a touch of the sight, we're expecting a girl."

Essie nodded as she crossed herself. "Ay, anyone blessed with the sight would know."

By the time I sat down with my coffee and a cup of tea for Charlie, the two ladies were busy talking nurseries and something called a layette. I drained half my cup before a break in their conversation.

"Excuse me, ladies. If I may be so bold, isn't it a little

early to be worrying about this? We haven't even been to the doctor yet. We're going on his brother's vision and his own wonky stomach."

Charlie lifted a finger. "And don't forget different foods have been smelling off to me."

The women nodded in tandem, while Essie patted my hand. "The signs are all there, Alpha. Your mate is pregnant, and it's never too early to plan."

Tina's eyes widened. "It really isn't, trust us. His pregnancy will fly by before we know it."

Shrugging, I reached for my cup again. "Then plan away. Let's get this figured out. I don't mind talking about our baby the whole day anyway, but especially when it puts the smile I'm seeing on Charlie's face right now."

When they both immediately turned to look at him, Charlie blushed, but his smile didn't fade. Tina scooted around and went for a hug, and for the first time, I noticed Charlie eagerly return her embrace.

ELEVEN

CHARLIE

About two months later...

Eli watched patiently while I walked back and forth with Stevie on my shoulder, rubbing his back and trying to calm him while the little guy screamed. With every step, my baby bump felt heavier, or maybe it was simply my sudden fear I was going to suck at this parenting gig. When I turned back his way, I looked at Eli in dismay.

"What am I doing wrong? I can't handle knowing your child's suffering because of something I did or didn't do. His diaper was changed, nothing was pinching, and I made sure his clothes were fitting properly. He drank the entire bottle, and I got a good burp. What does Stevie need that I'm not providing?"

As I held the baby out toward his father, silently begging him to take the poor tyke from my hands, Stevie's cry came to an abrupt halt. In its place came another burp, followed by a strange gurgling sound right before he spewed the contents of his bottle out like a fountain.

Not thinking to lower him in time, I took the hit directly

in the face. I wanted to gag from the taste—and knowledge—of regurgitated formula because of course I hadn't closed my mouth in time. Fluid poured off my face, dripping over my shirt and finally splashing onto the floor. Before I could react, Stevie started crying all over again.

My former best friend stared for half a second before laughing so hard he nearly fell out of his chair. Fortunately, Tom walked in the room. His special gift was healing. Stevie stopped crying the moment Tom cradled him in his arms. Rocking him back and forth, Tom brushed his fingers along Stevie's forehead and down his face, before gently pressing his stomach.

Taking a seat at the table and cooing at Stevie, Tom spread his hand out as his palm began glowing, as if lit from within by a soft white light. Retracing his original path, he gently brushed the glowing palm against the baby's head and cheeks and finally his stomach. By the time he was done, Stevie was sound asleep like an angel.

I grabbed a dish towel for my face and dropped down into the chair beside them, blotting the worst of the mess from my face and shirt while Eli and Tom talked. Or rather, Tom spoke, and Eli paid attention.

"He should be fine, now. He had the beginnings of an ear infection, and I think it was giving him a headache because he had tension all over his tiny scalp. Plus, his tummy was bothering him, and I noticed he was extra gassy. Have you considered switching formulas? I admit I don't know much about it, but I was looking at one of the baby magazines Charlie has lying around, and there was a whole article about the different brands. According to the article, the wrong formula can even affect their sleep patterns, making it harder for them to sleep through the night. Forgive me if I'm overstepping."

Eli whipped out his phone. "I'm making a note. Because you know what? This is silly, but I've been using the formula my papa used with my baby brother. I've accused Matt—jokingly, of course—how it's his fault Stevie won't sleep through the night. He never wakes me up, just rises when Stevie does and hangs out in the nursery for a couple hours, rocking Stevie while they share serious man talk. Whatever he means, right? For real, though, if changing his formula would help him sleep better, I am all over the idea. My poor alpha really needs to get more rest. I'm glad he and Stevie have bonded so well, but Matt has a lot on his plate."

"Let me grab the magazine. I'll show you the article. If it helps, then I'm glad I was able to suggest it." Tom started to rise, then stopped halfway up and glanced at the baby he was holding. "You mind if I take him with me? I hate to put him down when he's sleeping so well."

Waving his hand, Eli shook his head. "Mind if you take my baby and give me a break? Not at all. In fact, you can feel free to walk as slowly as you want."

Tom laughed softly, taking care not to wake the baby. "Tell you what, since we're only about a month away from having a baby in this house, I don't mind getting extra practice holding yours. There's a nice comfy rocking chair in Gidget's nursery. I bet Stevie would love if I made use of it while he sleeps. Come find me when you're ready to have him back."

As he slipped away with Stevie, Eli pouted at me. "You need to quit hoarding your brothers, Charlie. I think Tom would like a change in scenery, don't you? Lucerne Valley is so nice this time of year."

Even though he was joking, the thought of my brother with the healing touch leaving us made me frantic. "You can't take him. You saw what happened with Stevie.

Gidget's going to need a healer around here full-time with me as a parent."

Dropping all pretense and studying me with concern, Eli scooted closer and reached for my hand. "Oh, Charlie, no. For one thing, every baby is different. Which, considering, is probably why my brother's old brand of formula might not be the best choice for Stevie. I got a bunch of different samples in the mail after I started signing up for the free baby magazines. Am I a bad parent for not putting that together myself? No way. Because all any parent can ever do is their best. And let me tell you, what works today might not work tomorrow. Like Noah with different vegetables. The trick is to keep trying. Also, you heard Tom. Stevie had the beginnings of an ear infection, and his head hurt. No wonder he was crying."

"You might be right, but what about the part where Stevie stopped crying as soon as Tom took him? Tom hadn't used his healing touch yet. As for the gas, it might not be the formula. Maybe I didn't burp him right. You heard the noise he made before he puked on me." I hated to sound like a whiner, but I was seriously worried now.

"Charlie, quit fussing so much. Don't take Stevie's crying personally. You're a lovely person with a warm, caring heart, and your concern shows you're going to be a great dad. But if I can offer one tip? I learned this the hard way. Babies pick up on our tension. He calmed down for Tom because Tom wasn't stressed to the max. There will be nights, and days, where you will walk the floors with Gidget, and nothing will make her calm down until she magically passes out. Or, like we just witnessed, someone else comes along and has the perfect touch she'll need at the time. Ask anybody who's had a child—they'll tell you I'm correct."

His advice made sense. Wrinkling my nose at the foul taste in my mouth, I poured myself a fresh cup of tea from the pot I'd set on the table when Eli arrived and settled back to drink it. Eli warmed his own cup while he quietly let me absorb his words. As chatty as Eli could be, he was equally capable of enjoying the occasional comfort of silence. The closer we had gotten over the past few months, the more I came to realize what an amazing friend I'd been gifted through my mate. As I began to relax, I decided to open up about everything tearing me apart.

"I have been pretty stressed lately. It's not simply Gidget, although I am understandably nervous about becoming a parent. It's just been so much change, you know? For over twenty years, my life was a structured routine. Change came slowly, related to physical growth. If anything, our rules got stricter as we aged. Don't get me wrong, I don't miss the barn or anything about it. I'm glad those people are dead, and I don't have to worry about finding any forgiveness in my heart for what they did to me and my brothers. I also don't regret finding Lucian or bonding with him. I would want nothing at all about my life to be any different, except maybe I'd like to be a better son."

Holding his cup between his hands, Eli blew on the surface of the hot beverage before tilting his head with a curious frown. "What do you mean? Your mom was leaving when I got here, and you were making plans to bake bread with her tomorrow. Do you have secret voodoo dolls of them you stick with pins every night?"

"Funny. Actually, no, it's not. I'm pretty sure voodoo is real, and we shouldn't joke about it." I set my cup to the side and drummed my fingers against my leg as I sighed. "No, I feel bad because I still haven't started calling them Mom and Dad, even though I know they're dying to hear it. It took me a few to build a connection with them, and it's been getting stronger, especially with the pregnancy. But I don't have the same history with them my brothers do. As much as they want me to instantly be part of the family, I'll never fit in the same way as I should have. We don't share the same inside jokes or memories."

I felt like I was complaining, but venting everything I'd been holding in was such a relief. "The other day, Ford was talking about his grandmother who died a few years ago, and it took us a good twenty minutes to realize she was my grandmother too, even though I have no clue what she looked like or whose mother she was. Neither my brother nor I had thought about my connection to the lady until I pointed it out. Plus, how confusing is it for people when I talk about my brothers? I could be talking about my blood brothers, or I could be talking about my brothers of the heart, the ones who lived beside me my entire life, sharing the same miserable existence while we plotted ways to escape."

Eli gave me a no-nonsense glance. "For the brother thing, the word is siblings. Learn it and embrace it. If you refer to Ford and Colt as your siblings, and the other guys as your brothers, it'll solve any confusion. Okay, now it's time for real talk. Here's the thing, Charlie. Your parents know nothing was your fault. Press your hands to your baby bump. How many times a day do you feel Gidget kick? How often do you imagine what her face is going to look like, or, as we witnessed earlier, how worried are you about whether you'll do things right with her? Now imagine getting to the end of your pregnancy, only to have the doctor tell you she died. You never got a chance to hold her, to see her face and imprint it on your heart, nothing. After carrying her under your heart for four months, she's gone.

You find a way to move on, even going so far to risk another loss by getting pregnant again."

He had to stop for a second to grab a napkin, even passing one to me since we were both crying. Eli blew his nose like a foghorn before continuing. "Twenty years goes by. Then somehow, out of the blue, a grown-ass adult shows up and turns out to be your long-lost baby. Instead of being dead, you have a chance to hug Gidget and show her every drop of the love you've been holding in your heart for her. Now tell me, do you think Tina and Dave are worried about what you call them? Or whether you get their inside jokes? Sweetie, believe me when I say they don't give a darn about anything other than having a chance to love you. And now, you're even giving them a grandchild."

Wiping my eyes, I took a steadying breath before I attempted speech. "When you put it that way, I feel like an immature jerk. Now I want to run over to their house and smother them with hugs. By the goddess, I never considered it from their point of view. I was so busy feeling pressured by their immediate love and acceptance, when what I wanted at the time was to obsess over Lucian and enjoy being newly mated. It never occurred to me the amount of grief they must have felt or what a complete shock it was to find me alive and well."

"Don't get cocky. The jury is still out on how *well* you are. I mean, we still need to discuss the whole Gidget of it all. Are you seriously naming your child after an old Sandra Dee movie? What, are you picturing her growing up and hanging out at the beach with Moondoggie and The Big Kahuna?"

After I got done laughing, I wagged a finger in his general direction. "First, I'm absolutely naming her after the Sandra Dee movie because Gidget is not merely adorable but a good girl. Her actual name will be Francie, just like the character in the movie, but Gidget will be her nickname. Lucian approves, even after I made him watch the movies. And yes, I made him sit through every one of them."

Eli snorted so hard I'd swear I felt the blast of air. "No, honey. His behavior proves nothing except Lucian adores you, rightly so, and will do anything you ask. However, I forgot Gidget's actual name was Francie, which is cute, so I'll allow it. Even if I'm the only one who will probably ever use her full name."

"I hate you." I stuck my tongue out like a mature adult.

Naturally, Eli stuck his out in return. "No, you don't. I'm your bestie. So tell me, you feel better after getting your angst off your chest? You can always talk to me about anything, even if it feels silly at the time. And more importantly, you should be sharing these feelings with Lucian. Don't worry about weighing him down when he has a responsibility to the pack. We come first to our alphas, don't ever forget."

Shrugging, I started to lift my hands, then dropped them into my lap instead. "That's the thing, Eli. I didn't even realize this was festering inside. I've been so busy preparing for Gidget, and getting to know my family, and learning how to live with my other brothers gone while worrying about the ones I still have leaving and... I don't know. I guess I was pushing it down while I went about my life, and it came to a head. Aren't you glad you were here?"

I was being playful, but Eli smiled compassionately as he reached over to give my hand a squeeze. "I *am* glad. What are friends for? As for your brothers, I've got nothing because you have a unique situation. I guess be glad we live in an era of instant communication and video chatting, right? As much as you want to keep them all close, I know you wouldn't deny any of them the chance of finding the same happiness you found with Lucian."

"No, I really wouldn't. Okay, I'm going to go steal your baby back from Tom and give him a few kisses before you hit the road. If you want a few quiet moments to finish your tea, now's your chance." Eli laughed as I jumped up and left the room, but I noticed he didn't follow. I made a mental note to remember this moment and find my own chances to steal a few minutes of quiet when I had my own baby. And also? The next time I saw my parents, I was going to casually call them Mom and Dad.

Maybe if I didn't make a big deal out of it, we could make the name transition without it getting awkward. Then again, awkwardness was pretty much my thing. So... yeahhh. I was going to do it anyway. It was past time.

Two weeks later...

Tom finished polishing the wine glass he was holding before turning it upside down and sliding it into place. He gave the area a final look before nodding his approval. "Anything else, Charlie? I think these were the last item on the list, right?"

Rubbing my belly, I winced, shifting sideways on the stool when a sharp gas pain stabbed through my abdomen. "Yeah, we're only waiting for Darcy to finish stocking those brochures on the rack. Otherwise, the tasting room is good to go for tomorrow. Thank you both for helping me out today. I don't know what I would've done without you."

"No kidding, especially when you forgot to bring the checklist. We were lucky Raul noticed it on the table and brought it by." Most people would probably think a healer would be easygoing by nature. Not our Tom; he was as rigid as they came. I was pretty sure he had thrived in our old structure and routine.

Darcy looked over, rolling his eyes as we shared a grin. "Chill out, Tom. The list didn't have anything we couldn't have figured out with common sense. Serve wine with a smile and a clean glass. Done. Clean up after every group. Done. Restock everything at the end of the day. Done and done." Darcy laughed when Tom held his middle finger up, a gesture we'd all learned thanks to Colt.

"Hey, Charlie. I was mostly needling you. Darcy's right. We would've been fine without it. And by the way, quit thanking us because we were happy to help today. You didn't ask for the normal staff to get food poisoning because they shared bad tuna salad yesterday. With no one else available, why shouldn't we pitch in? I get you are the Alpha Mate, and you felt like it was your job, but you're about to have a baby. There was no way we were leaving you on your own. Besides, it was nice to feel useful." This time, Tom's sweeter side came out as he spoke.

"'Tom's not wrong, you know? It did feel good to be useful. Phoenix has somehow weaseled his way into a job in the laboratory. And we hardly ever see Kano since Lucian asked him to help with the irrigation problems." Darcy shoved a final handful of brochures into the wall holder, before crossing his arms over his chest. "You know what? If safe jobs could be found for those two, I'm sure we can do something around here. Tom's absolutely right—having a purpose today felt good."

When another pain hit me, Tom noticed my wince because he was facing me. He instantly came around and pressed his hands to my stomach with a far-off look in his eyes. After several seconds, he nodded to himself before dropping his hands. "I think it was gas. But you're getting close enough we need to pay attention. I know Dr. Diego warned about Braxton-Hicks contractions, but babies do come early. I'm not saying Gidget will, but we should definitely keep track."

A car door slammed outside, startling all three of us. Darcy clutched his stomach, then took a few steps away from the door, coming closer to us. "Reach out to Lucian. I don't know who's here, but it's not good. We need protection. I feel the danger so deep, it's in my bones."

I didn't hesitate, especially as the door began to open. *"Lucian! Are you nearby? Someone pulled up, and Darcy says we're in danger."*

He answered immediately without bothering to question whether he was truly needed. *"Are you still in the tasting room, or are you home? I'm in the middle and can be in either place in a couple minutes. I just need to know which way to run."*

"The tasting room. Hurry, charming. Darcy's gut is never wrong." The door opened, and the bright sun hitting me in the face temporarily blinded me after sitting all afternoon in this dimly lit room. Even though there were plenty of windows, the wood-paneled walls and leather stools made the place feel dark, despite the so-called romantic lighting. I couldn't make out anything about the shadowy figure in the open doorway, other than she was female. Or at least dressed femme. The door swung closed right as my eyes began to adjust, and I did a double take.

Despite being every bit as nervous as I was, Darcy took a protective stance in front of me, as if his small frame would help. "M-mistress? W-what are you doing—I mean...

H-how are you doing? It's been so long since we've seen you."

Tom came around the counter, confidently crossing the floor as if she was a normal customer dropping in. He snagged a brochure from the wall and tried to hand it to her. "As happy as we are to see you, I'm afraid you've caught us after-hours. Rules are rules, and if we bend them for anybody, we'll have to do it for everybody. So as much as it pains me, I'm afraid we'll have to invite you to come back tomorrow during our regular business day."

Her hand rested inside a big red purse hanging at her right hip, draping across her chest from the opposite shoulder. As her hand came out, metal gleamed before she even finished removing the gun. Batting away the brochure Tom was still holding, she removed the safety with a loud click. "I've heard quite enough rules for one lifetime, thank you very much. Now get over there with your friends, young man. I have some things to say."

Before we had a chance to find out what, the door swung open again, and two young guys came in. The younger one couldn't have been any younger than Colt, so figuring out who they were was easy. I'd like to say Josh appeared familiar, but I didn't remember enough about Two to recognize him. Alex somehow managed to look exactly as I pictured him, like an average guy in his early twenties with a pleasant face and brown hair. And kind eyes. He definitely had those.

Josh tried to say something to his mother, walking her over to one side of the room while Alex came closer with a curious, yet anxious, smile. "I'm sorry we interrupted you. Our mom hasn't been feeling her best. By any chance, would one of you happen to be known as Thirteen?"

Nudging Darcy with a poke in the side, I couldn't help

smiling at the friend who'd saved me, despite the tension in the room. Part of me was hoping keeping it might help defuse the situation. "You got me, although these days I go by Charlie. Since you didn't ask, I'll volunteer. I named myself after my favorite author Charles Dickens. I think we can agree Dickens would've been a horrible choice with awful nicknames nobody wants to hear."

Alex looked like he wanted to laugh but didn't dare. He'd always been so happy-go-lucky in our interactions. I couldn't help but wonder what the heck he'd been through in the past three and a half months. He swallowed, then managed another smile. "I'm glad you got out of there. I was so worried when I couldn't take you the whole way. Did Ford help you? I'm only guessing since you ended up with his pack."

"Surprisingly, not at all. Although I do have an ironic thing to share about Ford when we find time to really chat." The tension was getting thicker, and Josh and his mother were in the corner, exchanging a whispered argument. "And when we do, I'll tell you about how I met my true mate. Who, funnily enough, is the Alpha here. So yeah... my life completely changed. Thank you for not being dead. I was so scared when Jones fired his gun."

"You and me both, Thirt—ah, Charlie. It went down exactly like I told you it would. I shifted back, and Jones took one good look at me and freaked out. I meant to get in touch with you sooner, but I couldn't find the, uh, link we used. I guess I was out of range? And then Mom took us—"

His mother interrupted him. "No, Joshua. I know exactly what I'm doing. I don't need to take pills, and I don't need to go back to my silly doctor. I need to talk to the boy and find out where your father went. He's not dead. I would've felt it in my soul. You don't have to be someone's true mate to have a deep connection transcending time and space, you know."

Josh was muttering something, but I didn't have a chance to try to eavesdrop because the door flew open, and Lucian came striding in with my father and Pedro. Before any of us had a chance to process the new arrivals, Mistress surprised us all. Grabbing Josh's shoulder, she spun him around, then wrapped her arm around his neck, pulling him against her side and pressing the barrel of her gun to his temple. I knew she meant business. It was obvious in her cold, dead eyes.

Holding his hands up to show he was unarmed, Lucian edged toward her. "Ma'am, you don't want to do anything rash. Let's put down the gun and have a conversation."

Shaking her head, she snarled at my mate. "Back off. I was trying to have a conversation when my ungrateful boys interrupted, and now you and whoever those two are. How about everyone leaves and lets me finish my conversation with those omegas over there, huh?"

"I'm afraid I can't, ma'am. My mate is pregnant over there, and it's up to me keep him safe. We can have a conversation. I'm sure my mate will agree. But first, you need to put down the gun."

The gun slipped as she started yelling, but not enough to get Josh free from danger. "I'm not dropping my gun, and I'm not leaving. I'm done with people like you telling me what to do. Don't patronize me with half-truths and bold-faced lies. People lie to me all the time, and they think I can't scent it, like I have a broken sniffer or something. Second I drop this gun, you're going to forcibly drag me out and probably turn me over to the territory chief. No, I merely want to know where to find my husband, and I will be on my way."

Alex took a step toward her. "Mom, I told you I found his coroner's report online. Your mate is gone."

"Bullshit. Men like my Eggie don't die. And if he is gone, then someone killed him. I bet it was one of you, seeking revenge. Sure, he might've taken you, but you can't deny you had a soft life in a comfortable environment. Didn't I bring you a present every Christmas and a cupcake on your birthday? Did you ever lack for clothes or shoes? You even got movie night and a good education, thanks to my Eggie. I know because I kept an eye on things out there. The housekeeper reported to me regularly, which is why I know all about your little stunt, Alex. How you helped one of these ungrateful runts run away. Brought trouble into our lives."

Shaking his head, Alex turned back to me with a note of apology in his voice. "She had a mental breakdown after her mate sent us to a safehouse, and she found out later that our entire property had burned down. But we haven't been able to talk her into taking her pills or going back to the shrink."

"Liar!" Mistress released Josh, shoving him to the floor as she stepped forward, swinging the gun in a wide arc before pointing it at Alex. "And quit calling him my mate. Until you somehow managed to meet this filthy omega, you never hesitated to call him Dad. Especially when you were spending your father's money."

Alex stared down the barrel of the gun without backing off. "I will never call him my father again. He kidnapped a bunch of kids and kept them imprisoned in our barn. I've tried to protect you, but to see you standing here while you hold your own sons at gunpoint? I knew our family was fucked up, but I'm done. We need to leave these people alone and get out of here. I will drive you anywhere you need to go, but not with a gun in my face."

She sniffled loudly, shaking her head as crocodile tears began dripping down her cheeks. "Like I would really shoot one of my own babies. It doesn't matter how I got you. What matters is I was a good mom. The best. We gave you boys a perfect life, dammit. It can't end like this—it *can't*. No, the one who needs to die is the one who started all this by separating you from your family in the first place."

She turned the gun toward me and fired. Thankfully, the bullet went wide, and a shower of glass fell behind me. Without hesitation and a steady hand, she chambered the next round and lowered the gun slightly before firing again.

Alex jumped sideways, getting in front of the gun in time to take the bullet meant for me. He dropped with a thud, the coppery, fresh smell of blood filling the air. She screamed and started to chamber the next round, ignoring her son's injury.

A small gray wolf darted past and lunged at Mistress. He took her down, the gun falling to the floor. Lucian was already moving to take over when Tom finished her off, breaking her neck between his jaws.

Everything went silent as Tom lowered his head, pained to have to take a life, even in defense of mine. Given his healing abilities, I didn't doubt how difficult it must have been.

The silence was broken when Josh ran past her body, rushing to get to Alex. Kneeling beside his brother, he pressed his hands against the bright red bloom of blood on the right side of Alex's chest, begging for help. "I don't care about her dying, and I swear I wasn't part of anything they did. All we wanted was to get her to a hospital so we could escape and get away forever. Please, can someone help my brother? Don't let Alex die. He's all I have."

TWELVE

LUCIAN

Some might have thought it strange for Tom, the young, naked omega, to gently urge Josh aside so he could help Alex. Especially because he had recently taken the life of their supposed mother. But nobody in this room was one of those people. We knew the history and had watched it all go down. Fuck, having to stand here powerless while my pregnant mate was at the mercy of a crazed woman with a gun was undoubtedly the scariest moment of my life.

For once, I'd been unsure how to respond. I would have scooped Charlie into my arms and gotten him to safety without hesitation, but even going to him was risky. From the acrid stench coming off her, I knew the woman was ill. I just hadn't realized it was a mental health issue. I didn't know we could scent such conditions.

Tom ripped Alex's shirt open, his eyes closed as he probed a finger around the bullet wound. Since I knew he was about to use his healing powers, it occurred to me I should probably get people who weren't in the know out of here. I couldn't reach Charlie, not without stepping over Alex, which wasn't happening. I settled for our mental connection. *"I love you, beauty. It was horrible to see you in danger and not know how to best protect you."*

"I know, charming. I could feel your fear, and it made me sick at heart. Also, not gonna lie, I might've peed myself a little. Actually, I'm lying. I totally peed. If anyone notices, I'm blaming Gidget."

"And I will back you one hundred percent. Forgive me, but I need to clear the room so Tom can work. I'll be right here the whole time. I only wish I was there beside you."

"I know, but it's okay because you're here. Now go do your Alpha thing. You can fuss over me later."

I blew him a kiss, then remembered what I was doing. Starting with Pedro, I touched his arm and quietly passed my phone over. "Would you do me a favor, buddy? I need to hug my mate and make sure he's okay, not to mention keep an eye on things in here in case Tom needs help. The territory chief's number is in my contacts. Give Ash a call and ask him to hightail it over here, would you? He's been hunting for this woman, and he'll need to handle an investigation."

"Sí, Alpha. No problemo." With a wink, Pedro ducked out the door, making me wonder yet again precisely how much got past him and Essie.

When I turned to Dave, prepared to ask him to do something like track down Raul in the golf cart, Charlie interrupted with a knowing smile. "Lucian, unless you need my dad, I'd like him to stay. If he doesn't know about omega gifts, and if Josh and my brothers don't mind, I'd like to loop him in. Without my abduction, he and Mom would've known about it when I hit adolescence."

Shaking his head, Tom didn't glance away from Alex while he muttered he didn't care. Darcy shrugged, and Josh seemed curious. "What do you mean by gifts? You mean like how I can speak to animals and understand what every bark, meow, quack, and moo means? My so-called parents never believed me. They thought I was making up stories. Only Alex ever listened."

Charlie smiled fondly. "Explains why he was able to roll with my mindspeaking abilities. He never told me he had an omega for a brother. I didn't find out about you until after things went down. He played it off like he'd heard about omegas and understood they were rare. Your brother's a standup guy, Josh. No offense, but I think he's been protecting you from your parents for a lot longer than you know."

As for Dave, when Tom's hands began to glow, Dave's eyes widened as his mouth fell open. Especially when Tom plucked the bullet from his chest with a steady grip and pressed those still-glowing hands against the outside of the wound. His hands moved constantly, massaging the flesh while he worked his magic. The blood stopped pouring, and the flesh inside stitched itself together.

When his hands started to tremble, Darcy squeezed in behind him and rested his hands on his shoulders as if sharing his strength. Whatever it was, it seemed to be working because Tom's hands steadied again, and he was able to finish the job. Tom didn't relax until Alex began breathing normally, and his eyes moved under his lids. Tom glanced up at me. "Alpha, if you would be so kind, I need your help now."

"Anything, Tom." I wouldn't normally offer such a carte blanche response, but I knew in my gut Tom wouldn't ask me for more than what he absolutely needed and felt no one but me could provide.

Tom waited until Darcy scooted away before leaning back on his heels. "I need you to use your Alpha powers to force a shift. Shifting won't repair everything, but it will speed things along since I've healed his actual wound. After that, we need to feed him and pour him into a bed for some sleep."

Taking him at his word, I pushed a wave of power toward Alex, focusing only on him. "Alex, I'm calling your wolf forward. You are going to shift for me now." On the final word, I sent a double dose his way. Instantly, his body contorted and changed. Bones snapped and realigned while muscles and ligaments moved around like marbles in a flesh-colored bag. His teeth and fingernails lengthened, dark brown fur sprouting along his visible skin.

With a relieved laugh, Josh stood and took a step back. "We probably should've at least removed his jeans first. Now he's going to be naked and gross."

Tom glanced over his shoulder at Darcy. "There's a stack of tablecloths in the cabinet left of the sink. He can wrap up in one of those until someone finds him something to wear."

"I can run over to my place. I'm sure Ford has something. You said they were friends anyway, didn't you?" Dave glanced at Charlie for the last part.

Nodding, Charlie made his father's day with the first word out of his mouth. "Dad, what a perfect idea. Thank you."

Dave nearly melted on the spot. "Happy to help... son. And if I might say so, I'm especially glad to lend a hand to the young man who helped get you out of that place." He was already backing toward the door, his voice rough as he blinked several times. Muttering something about allergies, Dave rushed out of there with a promise to be back immediately.

Everything was a constant swirl of activity, and I still

didn't have Charlie in my arms. My wolf was getting pissed, and I was right there with him. I was about to offer to move Alex to a more comfortable spot when Tom sniffed the air and gave Charlie a closer look.

"Um, Charlie? Have you been having any more gas pains?"

Charlie turned pale as he nodded. Pressing both hands against the sides of his belly, he winced in pain. "The whole time we've been sitting here. I got a sharp one when she pulled out the gun, about the same time I peed my pants. They haven't stopped, either. It's gotten so bad. As soon as one passes, the next one starts."

"Darcy, grab more tablecloths." Tom didn't hesitate to start barking orders. "Josh, your brother is fine. I don't care how you do it, but I need you to move him over there to your right. Alpha, if you'd be so kind as to lift your mate onto the counter after Darcy spreads out a few tablecloths, I'd appreciate it."

Slapping at Tom's arm, Charlie looked completely panicked. "Tom, stop messing around. You almost made me think I'm in labor."

To his credit, Tom remained completely calm, rubbing Charlie's back. "Sweetie, you're in labor. You didn't pee yourself—your water broke. There was just too much going on for anyone to notice."

"Charming, I can't do this. Not here! I don't want Gidget born on the counter in the middle of the tasting room. Take me somewhere, anywhere."

Josh was struggling, since Alex had shifted back without waking. To simplify things, I lifted him and carried him over to the table Tom had pointed out, the furthest point in the room from their dead mother's body. However they'd come into her life, she'd raised them, and I couldn't imagine how rough this whole situation was for Josh and how Alex would feel when he woke up.

Move accomplished, I strode over to my mate and finally lifted him into my arms. Cradling him close, I kissed the top of his head while Darcy quickly finished preparing the counter. When I went to lay him down, Charlie clung to my neck, shaking his head. This time, he spoke aloud. "No, charming. I can't do this here. By the goddess, our customers drink our wines at this counter."

I wasn't sure how he'd react, but I actually had a good response. "And more than one of them haven't been able to handle their alcohol and proceeded to throw up on it. We'll do the same thing we do then—sanitize it and get it nice and clean for the next people who need to use it."

"Ew. And you want your daughter born where people puke?" Charlie started giggling, giving up the fight when Tom cleared his throat. "Fine, but try not to let anyone see. I've been pretty dang preggo lately, and I'm not sure how well the landscaping has held up, if you know what I mean."

His brothers both laughed at my answering growl. Rolling his eyes, Darcy lifted another tablecloth from the cabinet. "Charlie, in case you missed it, your mate is saying he doesn't want anyone looking at your precious bits any more than you do. Now let's get those pants off. I have a tablecloth to spread over your legs. Nobody will see your business but Tom. And we both know he'll be too laser-focused on performing the perfect delivery to notice anything else."

Tom nodded as he shrugged. "It's like they know me or something. Although I will go on record and say I told you so, Charlie. You said I was being overprepared when I studied how to deliver a baby and made you take me on your last doctor appointment so I could pick Dr. Diego's brain. See? I was trying to extend my knowledge, but now I can help you in your hour of need."

If he was attempting to distract Charlie, it worked beautifully. Charlie was too busy muttering about cocky, know-it-all brothers to pay attention as I carefully removed his pants and shoes. As promised, Darcy whisked the tablecloth right over him, forming a perfect barrier to satisfy Charlie's modesty—and my wolf's and my own need to keep prying eyes away from what was ours. I felt like a caveman, but there was no fighting natural instincts at a time like this.

Further distracting Charlie, Tom started his examination, asking Charlie to describe the pain and help him by watching the clock on the wall to see how far apart they were.

"Are you kidding me, Tom? A baby is about to come out of my body, and you want me to remember how to tell time?"

I was about to offer, but Tom shook his head. "Never mind, crybaby. Gidget is crowning. I can already see her head. Alpha, take Charlie's hands and help him push. Darcy, grab a clean tablecloth and get ready to take her." Tom talked Charlie through pushing as the next contraction hit. "Okay, good. Relax for as long as you can. I only have half of her head. On the next one, I need you to bear down with everything you've got and push like you haven't pooped in a week. Remember when we got punished and ate nothing but Brussels sprouts for two weeks? And how stopped up we were? Then you can understand the kind of pushing action I want to see."

This time, Charlie actually growled. "Tom, I love you with all my heart, and I appreciate you being here for me. But if you compare my daughter's birth to pooping one more time, I won't be responsible for what I do when this is over.

My payback will be slow and stealthy, and it will be filmed. Zero regrets. I will put it on TikTok for the entire world to enjoy."

"Got it, sweets. Babies aren't poop. You're going to destroy my life if I compare them again, blah blah blah. I see your stomach tightening, so here comes the contraction. Push, Charlie. Remember the Brussels sprouts!"

The door swung open, and Dave and Tina came in while Charlie pushed through the mother of all contractions, screaming in pain while somehow managing to laugh hysterically. I couldn't see what was happening under the tablecloth, so I kept my eyes on Charlie's red face. The door opened and closed again, but I couldn't be bothered to check. Not when my whole world was here on this counter. Charlie fell back against my arm, clutching my hand and panting with relief as a sharp cry filled the air.

Tom stood and looked around. "Alpha, it seems like Charlie needs you. Did you want me to go ahead and cut the cord?"

Shaking his head, Charlie answered before I could. "My parents are here. I want my dad to do it. He didn't get to cut mine. Maybe this will make up for it in some small way."

Dave had tears rolling down his cheeks as he came over with an extended claw. "Thank you, son. I know we stumbled in on this by accident, but I'm honored to be part of such an important moment." He gathered himself enough to cut the cord, then turned to pull a sobbing Tina into his arms. Tom passed our daughter to Darcy before muttering something about afterbirth and ducking back under the tablecloth.

"Not so fast." Charlie reached out. "Let me hold her, Darcy. I don't care how mucky she is. She is my little girl. If I learned anything from my own history, it's the importance of being able to imprint her face in my mind from the very start." As soon as he brought her close, he looked toward his parents with shining eyes. "She has our birthmark, Dad! Right here, it's the cutest little strawberry over her right eyebrow. Or, where her eyebrow will be since she doesn't seem to have any just yet."

"They're there, sweetheart. They're just more fuzz than hair at this stage." Tina smiled through happy tears, clearly as thrilled as we all were.

Charlie looked back at me. "Okay, it's time to do your part, charming."

It took me a moment to realize what he meant. Damned if I didn't have to blink a few times through blurry eyes before I could scratch an X over her itty-bitty heart with the claw I extended.

After we were done and ready to pass her back, Darcy held his hands up and stepped back. "I'm going to let your mom take it from here, Charlie. I'm sure she knows a lot more about cleaning a baby after birth than I do, and it'll mean so much more to her."

Bless Darcy for offering exactly what Charlie preferred since his parents were here and he could include them. Darcy had been up to bat originally because there was no other option. Not only was it the right thing to do—it was Charlie's way of closing the circle. Goddess, but I loved my mate.

Tina went from crying with shaky hands when she finally laid eyes on Gidget up close to steadying herself and becoming all business as she took the baby over to the sink and got to work. Dave hovered at her side, ready to pass her anything and everything she might need.

I was so busy watching them, mostly because I couldn't take my eyes off my baby girl, that Charlie caught me off guard, bursting out laughing. When I glanced back at him, he pointed toward the left-hand corner, where the dead body still lay. Ash was there, along with my buddy Nick and two men I didn't recognize, talking to Pedro, obviously already conducting his investigation.

I hoped Josh wasn't watching. Surprisingly, though, Alex was awake. The two brothers had their backs to their so-called mother's corpse, quietly talking while everything went on around them. I turned back to Charlie with wide eyes. "Am I dreaming, or is this the craziest day ever?"

"I was thinking the same thing. I'd offer to pinch you, but I'm too tired." He looked past me as the door opened again, smiling with relief when he saw Raul. "Oh, good. Our beta is here. He can take over the crazy in here, and we can confiscate the golf cart and go home. Mom can care for Gidget properly there while you help me take a hot bath."

Tom came around the counter, wiping freshly washed hands with a towel, shrugging at Charlie's lifted brow. "So I asked to share the sink for a second, sue me. And yes, a bath is a fantastic idea for you. You tore a little, but I healed you. You're good as new and ready for the next one."

Blanching, Charlie curled up against my chest, shaking his head. "There will be no talk of a next one until my brain has been able to recover from the multiple horrors of this one."

"Amen." I spoke without hesitation. It would be a long time before any of us got over this day.

Tapping my arm, Charlie whispered for me to help him back into his pants. Darcy and Tom chatted with him while I accomplished my mission. Tina and Dave turned around with a clean little angel cradled in Tina's arms, the moment after I helped Charlie sit up. He sat on the edge of the counter, swinging his legs and rolling his head from side to side as if working out the tension in his neck.

Tina offered Gidget, but Charlie shook his head. "You hold on to her for now, Mom. Keep her safe until I make it home. I was going to leave, but I think Lucian and I need to handle a couple things here before we head over. Raul can take you in the golf cart. You know where everything is in Gidget's nursery."

"It would be my honor, darling. My first grandbaby. You better know I will protect her with everything I have." Tina was crying again, but weren't we all?

Taking a moment to swipe his arm over his eyes, Charlie's Adam's apple bobbed as he swallowed. "Dang it, Mom. It's hard enough not to cry. Do you know how many hormones are flooding through my body? I'm a mess, I tell you. A complete mess. I'm worse than Bette Davis in every crying scene she's ever filmed."

His parents both laughed, smiling proudly first at Charlie, then me, before turning their adoring gazes back to our daughter. Charlie rested his chin on my shoulder. "Go ahead, Mom and Dad. Take our little girl home for me. Enjoy your granddaughter while you have the chance. Because after I get home and finally have my bath, I plan to be selfish while I count every finger and toe and take a million pictures."

Raul had obviously been paying attention because he came over with a smile and escorted Charlie's parents outside after taking a second to admire our daughter and congratulate us.

Meanwhile, the two strange men were wrapping the dead body while Ash and Nick chatted with the boys. And even better, Dave must have followed through on the promise of clothing because Alex was dressed.

Charlie tapped my shoulder. "Help me down, charming. I want to get in on their conversation."

When we arrived, there really wasn't much to hear. Ash was in the middle of explaining how their parents had brought them into the family. After both boys agreed to cheek swabs, they made it clear: while they were interested in finding their birth families, they would be sticking together.

Alex ended by looking to Charlie. "Charlie, I want to thank you for being so kind and not cussing me out for not telling you sooner who my family was the minute I walked in. At first, I didn't know it was important. And by the time I knew where you were and what it meant, I was afraid you wouldn't trust me if you knew. I planned to tell you after we got away, I swear. Josh was going to meet us on the way here, and we were going to ask Ford to introduce us to his Alpha."

I couldn't help chuckling when I heard, even though I was pretty sure Charlie had mentioned it himself at one point. Or maybe I'd filled in the blanks. "A friendly introduction would've been a better way than finding him half dead on the side of a ditch. But not how we were fated to meet. For the record, I would've welcomed you then, and I'm welcoming you now. Both of you will have a safe place and a pack if you want to stay here. Since you're already friends with Charlie and his siblings, I think you'd be a good fit."

With a respectful nod, Alex smiled. "I appreciate your offer, sir. And how funny is it that my friend Thirteen was my friend Ford's sibling this whole time? But I was talking to Alpha Nick, and I think I want to go back with him to the Newberry Springs pack. Josh and I need a change of scenery, and we're not afraid of hard work. I'll come visit in time. I'm sure Josh will too, but for now, we need to get far away from where we grew up."

Ash interrupted, clapping me on the shoulder. "Sorry, but I need to take off. Luckily for you, Nick and I were having lunch with Matt over in Mojave when Pedro called. I got the information I needed. This was a clean kill. Self-defense the whole way. Also, the deceased is a suspect in two ongoing investigations. I brought two of my men along. They'll deliver her to the state police, and our guys in blue will take over. I don't think anyone will bother you, but if they do, let me know, and I'll come out for the meeting."

He started to walk off, then turned back with an afterthought. "I can't believe I almost forgot. Congratulations on your little girl. Also, you can expect a trophy in the mail, if I don't deliver it myself."

"A trophy? What the hell did I win?" I scratched my head, desperately trying to remember if I entered any of the territory's silly little contests they ran from time to time.

Ash and Nick burst out laughing at the look on my face. Once he'd recovered, Ash grinned like anything. "What do you think? You and Charlie both earned the honor of the craziest birth story I've ever heard. Damn, I can't wait to start telling people. Hand to God, they'll swear I'm making it up."

"Don't worry, Ash. I've got your back. I took a few random shots to show everything happening in the room for my buddies." Nick held up a hand when I snarled. "Don't get your panties in a twist, Luci. Everything is tasteful. Nothing will make you want to punch me in the face. And if there is, I'll let the guys hold me down while you do it. Deal?"

Charlie answered for me, sticking his hand out to Nick. "Deal. You must be the West Coast Wolf brother I haven't met yet. If you don't mind, I'd like to see those pictures. As long as the dead body is blurred, I think those need to go in Gidget's scrapbook. I daresay it will be hard for anyone to have a better origin story."

Bypassing the outstretched hand, Nick shoved me aside and gave Charlie a big hug. "The guys told me I'd adore you on sight and how perfect you were for our Luci. I'm glad to know they were right about something for once. Usually, I'm the voice of reason. But you'll find out as much the more you get to know me."

"Fuck off," I snarled before bursting into laughter as I gave him a shove. "And quit hugging my mate. He's mine."

Nick stumbled back toward the counter, only to stop the dramatics as he froze and sniffed the air. "What is the amazing smell? Oh my God, it's like my Nana's butter pecan cookies and a shot of gin, rolled into one. Damn, it smells like home." He was completely fazed out, lost in whatever he was smiling at as he slowly turned.

Squealing softly, Charlie grabbed my arm and practically vibrated with happiness. An equally dazed Tom stared at Nick like he was the last donut in the box. If the box had been filled with his favorites.

Letting them have their moment, I spoke over our link. *"I hope you realize this means you're about to lose another brother, and even worse, our pack is losing our new healer."*

"Dammit. You're right. And I'm guessing I can't be selfish."

"Nope. And, since when do you cuss, beauty?"

"What can I say? My charming mate has a dirty mouth, and I learn things. You know what? Let's do these guys a solid and arrange for someone in the pack to drive Alex and Josh to Newberry Springs. Along with Tom's things. I have a feeling he's about to get on the back of the motor-

cycle I'm sure your friend rode up on and drive off into the sunset."

"Yeah, definitely. You know what? It couldn't happen to two better people. Tom and Nick will be great together, you'll see."

Charlie lifted a brow. *"Do you really think I'm going to question fate? After all, it gave me you."*

"Yeah, it did. And now you're stuck with me forever."

"Good thing I love you, charming."

"It really is, beauty. I'm the luckiest man in the world to have your love. And Charlie? I love you too."

Alex tapped me on the shoulder, motioning toward our friends, who were still stuck in a stare-off. "Umm, our car is right outside, and Alpha Nick already gave me directions. We were originally going to follow him, but I have a feeling we should go on ahead. Sound okay?"

"Yeah, go for it. He just found his true mate. He isn't going to be worth anything for the next little while. I'll get Alpha Matt from the neighboring pack to call the beta over in Newberry Springs and let them know to expect you. Promise not to be a stranger in the future, you hear me?"

They both nodded. When Alex hesitated, Charlie stepped forward to give him a hug. "I forgave you as soon as I realized why you probably hadn't told me. Forget about it. I already have. You've taken bullets meant for me twice now and saved my life both times. You've proven yourself to be my friend, Alex, and I don't take friendship lightly. I will always be there for anything you need. Reach out whenever."

Alex gave him another hug, then took a step toward the door. "Thank you, Charlie. I treasure your friendship as well. Rescuing you was probably the most important thing I've ever done. As for saving your life? I'd do it again in a heartbeat. But... maybe you could stop getting shot at instead?"

"No shit. You've got the right answer." Laughing, I waved as they left. I started to suggest we follow their lead, when I realized poor Darcy was still cleaning behind the counter. Glancing at Charlie, I subtly tipped my chin toward his brother.

Snickering, Charlie rolled his eyes. "Yo, Darcy. How about we give the lovebirds some space so they can stare at each other in private, huh? Come on. Essie has tamales put away. She said she was saving them for the day Gidget was born. And I have a bet to win."

My mouth was already watering. I was a tamale man from way back. If Essie's were even half as good as everything else from her kitchen, I was about to eat like a pig. With zero regrets.

Patting my stomach, I winked at my beauty. "Dammit, now I am gonna call her Mamá. Hey, you think if I do, she'll give me seconds?"

Charlie pretended to consider before shrugging. "Probably. I don't know, though, because first she has to pay off our bet. When she told me what she was serving, I told her you would react this way. And if that didn't do it, the Mexican street corn she's serving on the side definitely would."

As if completely appalled, I gasped. "You bet against your own mate? Your alpha, the love of your life?"

"Yep. And I'll probably do it again if I get the chance. Close your mouth, charming. You'll draw flies." He giggled, then bounced up on his toes to kiss my cheek. "Seriously, let's go. I need to get home to Gidget."

I didn't need any more reason to scoop him up and rush toward the door. Darcy laughed as he raced ahead of me, opening it wide for our big escape. And right as we walked out, damned if Raul didn't come flying around the corner, kicking up gravel as he skidded to a stop.

As we climbed into the golf cart, Charlie still cradled firmly against my chest, I nodded with approval. "Raul, you really are the perfect beta. A long time ago, I said I never wanted a pack, but you know what? I was wrong. This is my home now, and wild horses couldn't take you away from me."

Raul simply grinned, bringing two fingers to his forehead in a snappy salute. After a quick peek to make sure we were settled, he backed out and took off again, driving the damned golf cart like he stole it.

As we passed the now-empty fields where the current crop had recently been harvested, I looked out over my packlands with a grateful heart. Whatever her motivation, the goddess had really blessed me this year.

A perfect pack. An incredible mate. More family than I ever would've expected in this lifetime. And now, a precious princess of a daughter. Yep, I was going to need at least the next fifty or sixty years to count all my blessings.

Which suited me fine. With Charlie at my side, I'd live every one of those years knowing I was the luckiest bastard ever born.

ABOUT THE AUTHOR

Thank you for reading this book. Every story I write has a piece of my heart attached. Here's a little bit about me... I'm a happily married mom of one snarky teenage boy and three grown "kids of my heart." As a reader and big romance fan myself, I love sharing the stories of the different people who live in my imagination. My stories are filled with humor, a few tears, and the underlying message to never give up hope, even in the darkest of times, because life can change on a dime when you least expect it. This theme comes from a lifetime of lessons learned on my own hard journey through the pains of poverty, the loss of more loved ones than I'd care to count, and the struggles of living through chronic illnesses. Life can be hard, but it can also be good! Through it all, I've found that love, laughter, and family can make all the difference, and that's what I try to bring to every tale I tell.

Would you like to receive my newsletter?
bit.ly/SusiHawkeNewsletter

The Hawke's Nest is my Facebook reader group!
www.facebook.com/groups/TheHawkesNest

www.susihawke.com

facebook.com/SusiHawkeAuthor
twitter.com/SusiHawkeAuthor
instagram.com/susi.hawke
bookbub.com/authors/susi-hawke

ALSO BY SUSI HAWKE

Shifter Series

Northern Lodge Pack Series

Northern Pines Den Series

The Blood Legacy Chronicles

Legacy Warriors

Choose Your Fate

Assassin's Claws

Desert Homesteaders

West Coast Wolves

Co-Written Shifter Series

Waking the Dragons (with Piper Scott)

Team A.L.P.H.A. (with Crista Crown)

Alphabits (with Crista Crown)

The Family Novak (with Crista Crown)

Knotted Paths (with Crista Crown)

Non-Shifter Contemporary Mpreg Series

The Hollydale Omegas

MacIntosh Meadows

The Lone Star Brothers

Co-Written Omegaverse Series

Rent-a-Dom (with Piper Scott)

Three Hearts (with Harper B. Cole)

Standalone

Finding Sanctuary

―――

Contemporary MM Romance Series written as Susan Hawke

LOVESTRONG

Davey's Rules

News Boy

Realize (Men of Hidden Creek Season 4 Book 2)

Abandoning Ship

Dancing with Daddy

―――

Check out my audio books!

Susi Hawke on Audible

Susan Hawke on Audible

Printed in Great Britain
by Amazon